A Mutiny in Time

James Dashner

SCHOLASTIC INC.

For Dad, who showed me the magic of science
and the wonder of history
—J.D.

Copyright © 2012 by Scholastic Inc.

All rights reserved. Published by
Scholastic Inc., *Publishers since 1920.*
SCHOLASTIC, INFINITY RING, and associated logos
are trademarks and/or registered trademarks of Scholastic Inc.

No part of this publication may be reproduced, stored in a
retrieval system, or transmitted in any form or by any
means, electronic, mechanical, photocopying, recording,
or otherwise, without written permission of the publisher.
For information regarding permission, write to
Scholastic Inc., Attention: Permissions Department,
557 Broadway, New York, NY 10012.

Library of Congress Cataloging-in-Publication Data available

ISBN 978-0-545-62414-5
10 9 8 7 6 5 4 3 2   13 14 15 16 17

Cover illustration by Sammy Yuen
Cover design by Sammy Yuen and Keirsten Geise
Page design by Keirsten Geise
Back cover photography of characters by Michael Frost © Scholastic Inc.
Spanish coat of arms: Wikipedia/Proof02/GNV Free documentation license
Puzzle rendition of image: Keirsten Geise for Scholastic

This edition first printing, September 2013
Printed in the U.S.A.   40

Prologue

DAK SMYTH sat on his favorite branch of his favorite tree, right next to his favorite friend, Sera Froste. *Not a bad way to spend a Saturday afternoon*, he thought.

Beyond the safety of the tree, there was plenty to worry about. The world was falling apart and the people in charge of things didn't seem to care. But Dak decided not to let little stuff like that bother him now.

Sera apparently agreed. "Feels good up here," she said. "Doesn't it?"

"Yeah, it sure does. Makes me kinda sad I wasn't born a monkey. Then I could live in one of these things."

Sera laughed. "You've got the personality of a monkey. And the smell. That's two-thirds of the way there, at least."

"Thanks," Dak said, as if she'd just paid him a tremendous compliment.

A soft breeze made the branches sway back and forth, just enough to soothe Dak into a partial trance. He and Sera climbed up the tree every so often when there was nothing else to do. It gave them a chance to talk, away from any distractions—distractions like adults, who complained constantly about taxes and crime rates and, in whispers, about the SQ. With all the mental static, it was a wonder Dak and Sera managed to get any thinking done. Fortunately, they were both geniuses . . . although in very different ways.

"You excited for the field trip this week?" Sera asked.

Dak looked over at her, slightly suspicious. Their class was going to a museum, full of history — which he loved — and not a whole lot of science — which was her passion. But the question seemed genuine.

"Remember my last birthday?" he asked in return. "When I got that replica of Thomas Jefferson's ascot?"

"How could I forget? You came screaming down the street like a girl who'd just found a bucket full of candy."

Dak nodded, relishing the memory. "Well, I'm even more excited about this trip."

"Gotcha. That's pretty excited."

They sat in silence for a while, Dak enjoying the breeze and the sounds of nature and the break from the rest of life. Gradually, though, he realized that Sera seemed far less relaxed. There was an unmistakable tension in her shoulders that had nothing to do with tree climbing. He followed her gaze across the yard to his front porch, where his parents had recently put up a new flag. The small flagpole affixed to the side of the house was usually used for seasonal displays — holiday flags in the winter, the forty-eight-starred U.S. flag in the long summer months.

Now, for the first time, Dak's parents had put up a stark white flag with a black symbol in its center.

That symbol was a circle broken by a curve and a thunderbolt—the insignia of the SQ.

"Don't tell me your parents buy into all that," Sera said, her voice solemn.

"I don't think so. They said it's easier this way. They're less likely to be bothered if they just put up the flag."

"The SQ—they make me sick," Sera said. Dak had never heard such fierceness in her voice. "Someone has got to stand up to them eventually. Or someday it's going to be too late."

Dak listened to her as he stared out into the woods beyond his house. All that green, all those animals. There were parts of the world where these kinds of places had disappeared entirely. He'd read enough history to know that where the SQ went, trouble followed. He suddenly felt his own little burst of determination.

"Maybe it'll be us who stand up," he said. "You never know."

"Yeah?" she answered absently.

"There's an old saying," Dak told her. "The times, they are a-changin'."

"Ooh, I like that."

"Maybe that'll be our motto. Maybe we'll change the times someday. Every problem has a solution, right? And our big brains have got to be good for something. What do you say?"

She looked over at him and stuck out her hand. He shook it hard.

Somewhere nearby, a bird chirped excitedly.

The Only Hope

BRINT TAKASHI stared at the monitor and tried to remember a time when he didn't know the world was about to end.

Mari Rivera, his second-in-command, sat next to him, and the way she was slowly shaking her head back and forth, she seemed to be the second most depressed person on the planet. Brint was the first.

"Well?" Mari asked. "What do you think?"

"What do I think? I think we have a global catastrophe on our hands," Brint replied. "Volcanic eruptions all along the Pacific Rim. Blizzards in parts of South America that have never even seen snow before. If we're lucky, the tropical storm brewing in the Atlantic might put out the wildfires in the Northeast."

"Look on the bright side," Mari said, her voice grim. "At least people believe we're in trouble now."

"People still believe what the SQ tells them to believe. Because fear is always more powerful than truth." He ran his fingers through his dark hair and sighed. "Aristotle would be *so* proud. Look what the Hystorians have been reduced to! The SQ is going to win—even if it means destroying the world."

It wasn't just the natural disasters that had him worried. Or the blackouts. Or the food shortages. There were also the Remnants. Every day when Brint went home and looked at the picture that hung above the fireplace—he and his wife sitting by a river, the sun glinting off the water behind them—he felt a disorienting twist in his head and stomach. A gnawing gap in his mind that made him extremely uncomfortable. Someone—at least one someone—was *missing* from that photo. It made no sense whatsoever, but he knew in his bones that someone was missing.

He wasn't alone in suffering these types of sensations. More people experienced Remnants with each passing day. They'd strike when you least expected them. And they could drive you crazy. Literally crazy.

Time had gone wrong—this is what the Hystorians believed. And if things were beyond fixing now, there was only one hope left . . . to go back in time and fix the past instead.

Mari did what she always did when he was inclined to whine. She ignored him and moved on to the task at hand. "What's the latest on the Smyths?" she asked. Of all the scientists the Hystorians tracked, they were the only ones who hadn't been shut down by the SQ . . . yet.

Brint pulled up their file and pointed out the latest developments. All of the Smyths' experiments, findings, data—every little thing they did in their lab each and every day—it was all being monitored by the Hystorians. Without the Smyths' knowledge, of course. Brint would be sure to apologize for that *after* they saved the world.

They both fell silent for a minute, staring at the data on the screen as if hypnotized. The Smyths were so close. If only they could figure out the missing piece in their calculations. If only they could give the Hystorians a fighting chance at carrying out Aristotle's two-thousand-year-old plan to save the world.

"It's coming, you know," Mari whispered. "Sooner than I ever thought."

Brint nodded as dread squeezed his heart. "I never would've guessed it would be in our lifetime."

Mari continued, her words like a prophecy of doom from a wrinkled old oracle.

"It's coming, all right. The Cataclysm is coming, and we'll all wish we were dead long before it kills us."

2

Old Man in a Coffin

DAK SMYTH was a nerd.

He'd been called worse, no doubt. Dork, geek, wimp, brainiac, pencil-pusher, dweeb, you name it. But the word that most often floated out of people's mouths when they mentioned him was *nerd*. And did he mind? No. When all those dummies who poked fun were working their tails off in thirty years, living paycheck to paycheck to buy doughnuts and milk, he'd be laughing it up in his private jet, drinking cream soda till he puked. Then he'd laugh again as his butler cleaned it up, and when that was done, he'd count all his money and eat big blocks of cheese.

(Dak Smyth was a nerd who also loved cheese. Unnaturally so. Not a winning combination, which he was the first to admit.)

On the day before the big school field trip to the Smithsonian Museum in the nation's capital of Philadelphia, Dak had to put aside his nerd-powered excitement to attend the most boring of events—an uncle's funeral. Make that great-uncle, as in Great-Uncle Frankie, a man he'd laid eyes on all of twice if you included the viewing before the funeral, which Dak certainly did. He'd looked down on an old, grizzled man who had his eyes closed, hands crossed over his chest, looking like he'd just settled down for one of the twenty naps a day the geezer was probably used to. But, according to Dak's mom — and supported by the fact that the man was lying inside a coffin — Great-Uncle Frankie was dead as a doornail.

The funeral service had been slightly boring and lasted roughly one hundred and thirty hours, but now they were finally at the family dinner that came afterward. Dozens of people who'd been boo-hooing their eyeballs out an hour earlier were laughing like overcaffeinated hyenas, stuffing their faces with a whole week's worth of SQ-rationed food. Dak wondered whether funerals for old people always ended up being such festive affairs.

He sat at a table with a bunch of cousins, none of whom he'd ever met. They were talking about all kinds of things that he didn't care about. Like that lame show where they crown the next SQ intern. Or game five of some sports championship that was so dull Dak didn't even know which teams were playing (or what sport it was). Then some kid with a pimple the size of President McClellan's face on Mount Rushmore started talking excitedly about the latest fashion trends, namely those jeans with the pockets that made your rear end look like it was upside down. *Seriously?* Dak thought. These people couldn't possibly share the same genetics with him, could they?

Just as he decided he couldn't take any more, a sudden feeling came over him—a familiar itch that he'd learned long ago was impossible to ignore.

He *had* to share his tremendous knowledge of history, and he had to do it *now*.

Dak stood up and cleared his throat. When no one paid him any attention, he picked up his glass and tapped it loudly with his spoon until everyone in the room finally shut their yappers and looked at him.

"I just have something I'd like to say to everybody," he announced. He heard a few groans in response, but he assumed those were the old fogies, feeling aches and pains as they shifted in their seats. A quick glance at his mom showed that she'd put her head in her hands, and his dad was looking at him wide-eyed, slowly shaking his head back and forth. There was something like panic on his face.

Dak hurried to continue before somebody forced him to stop. "I know we're gathered here for a very solemn occasion. Poor Great-Uncle Frankie has gone the way of the dodo bird, soon to rot in peace. Um, I mean, rest in peace. But, um, I wanted to share something to help you all realize that things aren't as bad as they seem."

He paused to gauge people's reactions. They all seemed enraptured.

"You see," he continued, "our dear relative could've gone out the same way as Rasputin, the grand Russian mystic, in the year 1916. That poor man was poisoned, shot four times, clubbed over the head, then drowned in a river. Drowned in a river, for crying out loud! After being poisoned, shot, and clubbed! Poor fella." Dak let out a little chuckle to set the right mood. "So, as you can clearly see, Great-Uncle Frankie got off pretty easy when all is said and done."

Dak finished by pulling in a long, satisfied breath. He looked around the room and saw nothing but blank faces staring back at him. Lots of blinking.

"Thanks for listening," he finally said. Then he held up his water glass and yelled, "Cheers!"

His mom fell out of her chair.

The next day brought the field trip he'd been looking forward to for months. For someone who loved history as much as Dak did, going to the Smithsonian was better than getting locked in a candy factory overnight. He planned to gorge himself on information.

On the bus ride there, he sat by his best friend in the whole wide world. Her name was Sera Froste, and so far no one had given them any flack about being such good friends. Well, except for the occasional "when're you gonna get married" jokes. And the "Dak and Sera, sittin' in a tree" songs.

Okay, so they'd received plenty of flack.

"What exhibits are we going to see before lunch?" Dak asked her after he'd gone over the museum's floor plan with fluorescent highlighters. "And which ones after?"

Sera looked up from the electronic book that she was reading on her SQuare tablet, fixing him with the sort of stare she usually reserved for a bug in a jar. Her long dark hair made her expression look even more severe, as if it were on display in a picture frame. "Would you relax? Let's just play it by ear, roam around. I don't know, actually *enjoy* ourselves."

Dak's mouth dropped open. "Are you *insane*?" And he really meant it—she obviously didn't comprehend the opportunity they were about to be given. "We need to plan this to the second—I'm not taking any chance of missing something cool."

"Oh, for the love of mincemeat," was her only response before she returned her attention to *String Theory and Other Quantum Leaps in Quantum Physics.*

Sera was a nerd in her own right, almost nerdy enough in stature to compete with Dak himself. *Oh, who am I kidding?* Dak thought. She had him beat by a mile.

This was the girl who had recently convinced him to attend a Saturday afternoon thesis reading at the local university—"convinced" him by threatening to scream out in the middle of lunch that she was in love with him if he said no. Dak had fiercely protested because he'd wanted to see the guy at the state fair who swore he was so old that he'd been Mussolini's foot doctor during World War Two. (The man evidently had toenail clippings to prove it.) But Sera *swore* that it'd be more exciting to hear a three-hour presentation called "The Effect of Tachyon Generation on Ambient Wellsian Radiation."

It wasn't.

Sera had finally agreed to leave the presentation early, but only because the speaker kept using the words *baryon* and *meson* interchangeably when, according to Sera, everyone knows that's not proper.

Suddenly Dak had an idea. He ran his fingers through his sandy blond hair and stared intently at his color-coded floor plan. "I guess we can skip the Hope Diamond exhibit if we're short on time. It's supposed to be cursed, which is cool. I'm not sure what it means by 'an exploration of the biogeochemical processes that give minerals their unique properties,' though. It sounds like a total snooze fest if you ask me."

"Who asked you?" said Sera, putting her SQuare down. "Let me see that map."

By the time Dak and Sera marched off the bus, Dak's heart was giddy with excitement.

They had two hours and forty-seven minutes before the earthquake that would almost kill them.

Halls of Boring Wonder

POOR DAK, Sera thought as she and her classmates filed through the entrance to the Smithsonian. Her best friend was always annoying people with his ill-timed speeches on useless historical facts. And his obsession with cheese was just . . . well, weird.

Last year in fourth grade he'd written an entire poem about types of cheeses and how each one of them was like a family member to him. Mrs. E'Brien had finally relented and let him recite it to the class in exchange for his promise to spare them any spontaneous sermons about people who were dead. He'd proudly done his performance, but then only made it a day and a half before he suddenly blurted out a five-minute informa-tion dump about the guy who invented the stepladder.

So yeah, Dak was quaint and unique and a little bit annoying in his own quaint, unique way. But none of these qualities were what made Sera think *Poor Dak* that morning. What worried her was how clueless he seemed to be about the true state of the world.

The SQ. The natural disasters. The ever-increasing crime rates.

The Remnants.

That last thought made her pause, a deep ache pressing against her heart. . . .

And then the stinky kid named Roberk bumped into her from behind.

She knew it was him because an untimely draft pushed the boy's patented smell across her body like rotten air escaping from a newly unsealed tomb. The odor itself was a one-of-a-kind mixture of fried liver and boiled cabbage—it definitely put her in mind of hydrogen sulfide. "Geez, Sera," he said. "If you want a hug, just ask for it."

Sera wanted to tell him all about hydrogen sulfide, about how it was usually produced by swamps and sewage, which basically made Roberk a walking sewer—but it was hard to say anything while holding her breath. So she just gave him the biggest eye roll she could muster, then continued walking. She caught up to Dak in the atrium of the building, where the exhibits began on the other side of a huge open archway. Dak was craning his neck so much she thought he might strain a muscle. He was obviously dying to see what awaited them in the museum.

"Don't hurt yourself, there," she leaned over and said to him, determined to slam a door on the sour mood that had crept up on her when she'd thought of the Remnants. "You'll miss the whole tour if they have to take you away for emergency neck replacement."

"Whoa!" he whispered back fiercely. "I think that's a Viking longship in the next room! Must be a new exhibit. Do you think it's a karvi or a busse?"

Sera got on her tiptoes to look—through the archway she could see the ornate carved dragon head at the bow of what had to be a massive wooden ship. "Cool." She would've said more, but Mr. Davedson had just cleared his throat to get the class's attention. Their teacher was an odd duck—the word *crooked* described his features the best. Hair, eyebrows, mustache, ears, tie, pants. Everything about him seemed to lean to the left.

"Okay, kids, listen up!" He always called them kids, and she'd been tempted for months to respond, "Yes, Grandpa?" But she hadn't gotten up the nerve quite yet.

"We've got an awful lot of things to see today, and not much time to do it. Remember not to question the docent when he speaks—he's a representative of our beloved SQ." He shot a nervous look at a tall, smartly dressed bald man standing by the door. Sera had seen him when she'd come in, but she hadn't noticed the silver SQ insignia he wore on the lapel of his suit. "I expect everyone to be on their best behavior—in tip-top shape and proudly representing the fine institution of Benedict Arnold Middle School! Can I have a woo-hoo?"

Oh, please, Sera thought in a panic. Not this—not in front of the museum staff!

When no one responded, Mr. Davedson cupped his hand behind his ear. "I can't heaaaaaar you. Can I have a woo-hoo?"

The class halfheartedly gave him his lame cheer, and

he shook his head sadly. "Well, I would've thought we'd be just a little bit more excited to come here during such dark times. The SQ has graciously released funds to ensure the continued operations of this museum, and we should all be grateful!" He shot a second nervous glance at the docent.

That was another thing that made Sera want to scream. Not only had she gotten the biggest goon at the school as her teacher, but he always said stuff like that about the SQ. It was ridiculous to her that they should thank the SQ for not closing down a public building. As if anything they did could make up for the way they bullied the governments of the world. Not that she should expect her teacher to grow a backbone when even the President of the United States was eating out of the SQ's hand.

"Good ole Mr. Davedson," Dak whispered to her. "Can't say a bad word about anyone. You gotta love that guy."

Sera smiled despite herself. Dak was oblivious, but somehow he always saw the positive in other people. Even if it did annoy her sometimes, it was a trait she wished she had.

The museum docent, stiff and gruff and chrome-domed, finally took over command, paying further lip service to the SQ for "visionary leadership in trying times." Sera managed to suppress her eye roll until the docent had turned to escort the fidgety group through the huge archway and into the Age of Exploration exhibit hall. The longship Dak had spotted now loomed above

Sera like a hovering spaceship, suspended by almost invisible wires. Naturally, the group stopped walking right when she stood in its shadow. One little snap of a wire and she'd be crushed, her head ending up right next to her toes.

The room was filled with other replica boats, an early compass, a detailed diagram showing the difference between Viking and Egyptian vessels, and (of course) dust. Lots of dust. As the docent started droning on about this and that and who said what about who did that, she had the sudden realization that this could end up being the longest day of her life. She ached for the cool halls and auditorium of the local university. There was science and technology on display here, but it was hardly cutting edge.

On the other hand, Dak stared with fascination at the SQ puppet preaching his boring knowledge. He couldn't have been more riveted if a corpse had just dug its way out of a grave and started dancing. Half to annoy him, Sera nudged him with an elbow.

"So much for your step-by-step agenda," she said under her breath. "Looks like we're stuck with a babysitter."

Without looking at her, he whispered, "Yeah, this is some fascinating stuff. I can hardly believe I'm here to see it with my own eyes."

Sera realized it would be pointless to even try talking to Dak until lunch.

They moved on from there to other rooms and halls, learning about everything from dinosaurs to the SQ's influence on the space race. Sera tried to question something the docent said at one point, but her teacher hushed her immediately, once again looking around nervously.

Ugh, Sera thought. She swore to quit listening altogether.

Every once in a while, Dak would tear his gaze away from the docent and look at her with wide eyes. Then he'd say something like, "Isn't that cool?" or "Can you *believe* that?" or "Man, those Mongols had a sense of humor." She'd simply nod and hope he didn't force her to admit she hadn't heard a word that had been said.

Eventually they circled back and found themselves in the Exploration hall again, where they stood for what seemed like hours before an exhibit dedicated to the discovery of the Americas by the famous Amancio brothers. Everybody knew the story, though the docent left out the best part—the grisly fate of the cruel man that the heroically mutinous brothers had disposed of, Christopher Columbus. In fact, Sera had only ever heard of Columbus because Dak liked to tell the story. The man's name never came up in class or during Amancio Day celebrations.

The docent was just going off about how important the SQ had been in shaping the history of the world for the better when Dak cleared his throat loudly and raised his hand. *Oh, no*, Sera thought. *Here we go.*

"Excuse me!" Dak practically shouted when neither of the adults acknowledged him. "Excuse me! I have something important to say!"

Both men looked sharply at him.

"What *is* it?" Mr. Davedson asked. Sera knew that expression and that tone. The man had seen this happen far too many times — and he knew that indulging Dak at the museum could spell disaster.

"Well, I think you've *clearly* forgotten to say something important about the compass and its history." He let out a chuckle and glanced around the room as if all the students would be nodding their heads vigorously in agreement. When no one did, he frowned. "You know. How the fourth-century writings of Wang Xu in China were instrumental — pardon the pun — to the eventual discovery of magnetism and the directional iron needle. Heh heh. Hard to believe there was ever a world where people didn't know about *that*!"

The room had fallen tomb silent. Tomb-buried-under-three-miles-of-bedrock-under-the-ocean silent.

Someone sniffled.

Dak chuckled again. "Oh, man. Crazy stuff." He shot an embarrassed look at Sera then looked down at the floor, his face awash in red.

And those were the moments Sera realized exactly why they were such good friends. They were both inhumanly dorky. No judgments. She reached out and punched him lightly on the arm.

"Ow," he said. But he smiled, and the red in his cheeks started to fade.

"All righty then," Mr. Davedson barked, clapping his hands once. "That wasn't so bad. Let's all gather —"

A sudden burst of violent movement cut him off. The entire building started to shake, along with everything inside of it, display cases shuddering as the great hallway seemed to bounce and tilt and wobble. Screams erupted from every direction at once. Sera planted her feet and fought to keep her balance while most of her classmates fell on top of one another. Dak was one of them, tangled up in a sea of arms and legs.

As if anyone needed to hear it, Mr. Davedson screeched one word at the top of his lungs:

"Eeeeeeearthquaaaaaaaake!"

Cracks and Snaps

DAK KNEW very well that time made no sense during natural disasters—he'd been through a dozen or so over the course of his life. But as the terrible shaking of the world around him stretched on and on, he could have sworn that each second lasted a full minute. Terror filled his every muscle, bone, and nerve.

He currently had a foot in his mouth, and he was pretty sure it was Makiko's, her toe somehow squirming its way between his lips as a whole group of people tried to wrestle free of one another on the floor. He swatted her leg away just as someone's armpit replaced it, smashing against his nose. The ground beneath them felt like a nightmarish seesaw, pitching back and forth as the groans and squeals of bending wood and metal filled the air.

A hand suddenly slapped his back and squeezed the material of his shirt into a fist. Then he was yanked up to his feet. He spun around to see Sera staring at him with fear in her eyes. Somehow she'd turned into Marvelman when the quake started.

They stumbled away from the mass of kids on the floor to an open area that wasn't beneath any hanging displays, then helped each other maintain their balance as they staggered two or three steps one way then back the other. He saw an ancient Mayan figurine suddenly roll across the floor from another room, just in time to get stepped on and smashed by Roberk. Dak's heart broke a little, but a fresh jolt that threw him several inches off the floor brought him back to reality — he had to hope *people* didn't get smashed like that, too.

"It'll be over soon!" he yelled at Sera.

"If we don't die first!" she called back.

"Well, it'll end whether we die or not!"

"Thanks. I didn't know!"

A sudden *crack* rang out, a splinter of thunder that made the hair on the back of Dak's neck stand up. The sound had come from directly beneath them. He stared in horror as the ground split open before his eyes, a gap slicing across the floor like a zigzagging snake. Chunks of tile tore free and plummeted into a dark basement far below. Dak grabbed Sera by the arm and they jumped to safety, then watched as their classmates scrambled to get clear.

Two of their friends didn't quite make it. They dangled over the abyss, holding on for dear life. Mr. Davedson and the docent were sprawled out on the other side of the room and seemed to have no intention of helping the endangered kids.

"Get them!" Sera yelled, already moving.

Dak followed her as best he could — the building continued to tremble and shake, making it impossible to walk. They dropped to their knees and crawled forward to Makiko, who gripped a jagged outcropping of tiled floor. Her eyes caught Dak's, pleading for him to save her.

"I've got her!" he yelled at Sera. "Go help Fraderick!"

As Sera crawled away, Dak was left hoping he hadn't spoken too soon. If the building pitched at the wrong moment, he could slide right past Makiko and into the abyss below—probably taking her with him. He lay on his stomach to get as much stability as he could. Then he reached out and grabbed both of her arms.

He pulled, trying to bend his elbows and lift her out of the hole. She hadn't seemed very big whenever he'd looked at her before, but now she felt as if she weighed as much as Fat Bobby—that dude who sat in front of the Laundromat doing absolutely nothing on Saturdays. Dak screamed with the effort, throwing all of his strength into it. Makiko seemed to realize it wasn't working and started to climb him like a ladder, using his armpits and belt as rungs and the back of his neck as a foothold. He gurgled in pain as she lurched up and over the edge then toppled off of his body.

"Thanks, Dak," she said, facing him. "You're my hero." Then she giggled.

Dak could only stare at her. That was one messed-up girl.

He saw that Sera had gotten Fraderick pulled up safely as well, and everyone scooted as far away from the gap as possible. The building continued to shake, creaking and groaning all the while. But the hole in the floor had stopped growing. No one was screaming anymore.

We're going to make it, Dak thought.

Then something snapped, like a loosed rubber band cracking through the air. Then again. Then again.

"Up there!" someone yelled.

Dak looked toward the ceiling and saw that the thin wires holding the Viking ship upright were breaking free from the walls, whipping out to smack into the wooden craft. Its port side abruptly tilted downward several feet, sending a spray of broken drywall snowing down on top of the crowd. Shouts and screams again filled the air as everyone half-staggered, half-crawled out of harm's way.

He rejoined Sera as they moved toward the far wall. They were still a dozen feet away from safety when the floor lurched upward several feet then slammed back down again, as if the whole building had been picked up and dropped. Sera sprawled onto the floor as more *snaps* and *cracks* whipped through the air — this time followed by a terrible, creaking groan. The ship had torn loose and was tilting away from its perch, falling toward the ground as its final supports broke free.

Dak could see where it was headed and wasted no time thinking. He grabbed Sera by the hands and yanked her across the floor so hard that she slid ten feet and slammed into the wall. Then he dove after her. He didn't have to look because he heard it well enough — the ship crashed into the ground right where he and his best friend had just been.

And as if that had been nature's exclamation point on the whole affair, the earthquake ceased a few seconds later, everything almost instantly growing still. Dak twisted around to sit with his back against the wall, right next to Sera, who was pulling in heavy breaths, just as he was. They both stared at the smashed ancient long-boat, now nothing but a pile of firewood with a carved dragon's head sticking out at the top. Dak felt as if he'd just watched history itself being shattered.

"That was close," Sera whispered.

"Yeah," Dak agreed. "Good thing you have someone watching out for you. I'll take your thank-you payment in cash, credit, or fine cheeses. Your choice. I just wish I could've done something about that poor boat."

Sera shoved him gently. "If it was a choice between me or the boat, I'm okay with how it turned out."

Mr. Davedson was the first one to stand up, and he walked around the broken ship toward the large crack in the floor, brushing dust and debris off of his shirt and pants. He reached the edge and looked down, then turned to face the students crowded up against the wall.

"I can't believe it," their teacher said in a dazed whisper. "I just can't believe it."

"What?" Dak asked.

Mr. Davedson shook his head slowly back and forth. "Seven earthquakes this month. And now they're happening *here*."

No one responded, and his words hung there for a moment.

"The SQ has everything under control," the dust-covered docent insisted harshly.

Dak and Sera exchanged a quick glance. They'd never admit it aloud, but they couldn't quite believe him.

5

False Memory

THREE DAYS later, Sera suffered one of the worst Remnants of her life.

Her uncle Diego was out running errands, so Sera was home alone when she had an overpowering disturbance inside her head. An uncomfortable itch that made her stop and rub her temples, as if she hoped to dig deep down enough to massage it out. She couldn't explain it—she never could—but she knew with absolute certainty that she needed to go outside, to the backyard and fields behind her home, and walk to the old barn that was half a mile down the old dirt lane.

The sun shone in a sky without any clouds, but a grainy haze darkened the light to an orange glow, surreal and otherworldly. The haze came from forest fires in rural Pennsylvania, their fog of smoke drifting toward the sea on a light breeze like a noxious storm. Sera ran along the lane, enjoying the warmth despite the weirdness that had settled inside her, that pull to run to the barn for the umpteenth time in her life.

So she ran harder.

Dust billowed up from her footsteps and stuck to the sweat that had broken out on her legs. The dry heat nearly sucked her breath away. As she made her way down the lane, she thought of the earthquake at the museum and the SQ officials who'd insisted it was no big deal and all the other things that seemed to be wrong with the world. She also thought of Dak, her BFF Forever (which was redundant, but she still liked to say it that way) and how something deep inside her felt that there was a reason for their friendship. That something great waited on the horizon of their lives.

She reached the little grassy meadow that circled the barn, and stopped in the same spot she always did. A single granite boulder had stood there longer than anyone could remember—it probably went all the way back to the Precambrian age. It would probably outlast people. Leaning against it, Sera stared at the barn's warped wooden slats and the faded red paint that flaked away a little more with each passing year. And then she waited.

She waited for the Remnant.

There was a part of her—a rational side—that knew she didn't have to do this. That she could choose to ignore the craving to come here, could go do something else, avoiding the pain that was about to envelop her. But in some ways she welcomed the pain. Did she understand it? No. Did she enjoy it? No. But she welcomed and relished it because she knew it had something to do with a life that should've been. She knew it like she knew her hands were connected to her arms. And she couldn't pass up the only opportunities she'd ever have to experience it. Not even if it hurt.

And so, she kept waiting.

It began just a few minutes later.

There was a rushing behind her ears, within her head—a pressure that wasn't audible but was there all the same. An ache pierced her heart, a sadness that opened like a gate within her, a gaping maw of darkness that wanted to suck the life out of her and pull it down to the depths. She stared at the double barn doors, and even though they didn't budge, every part of her yearned for them to do so. She could almost see it, could almost feel the breeze that would stir as they swung open and slammed against the side of the barn.

Nothing happened, of course. But something should have. Those doors should have opened and two people should have walked through, calling her name with smiles on their faces.

Sera didn't understand it. She didn't understand it in the slightest.

But she knew. Those two people were her parents.

She'd never met them, and she never would.

6

An Iron Door

THE FIRST thing Sera wanted to do when the Remnant faded was go tell Dak about it. She always did. He himself had never experienced a major one—nothing that couldn't be explained away as déjà vu or a simple forgotten memory—so he didn't totally understand. But he tried to, and for her that was good enough. Plus, his parents were out of town for the weekend, so she knew he could use the company. Usually his grandma came over when his parents were gone, but she was older than most trees and spoke about as often as one.

Dak was in a lawn chair when she arrived, sitting under the branches of an apple tree as he read from a gigantic book. Normal people used their SQuare for such a thing, but not Dak. He'd search every library in town until he found the printed version of what he wanted, no matter how old it was or how battered.

"What're you reading?" she asked him.

He didn't answer, his nose buried in the pages and his eyes' focused stare moving across and down, across and down. This was classic Dak. She waited a few seconds

29

to be polite, then kicked him in the shin.

"Ow!" he yelled. The book slipped out of his hands and tumbled off the chair to land in a heap of brown leather and torn paper. The book was so old it had completely fallen apart.

"Oops!" Sera said. "Sorry. That's why you should do your reading on a SQuare."

"Yeah, because it'd be way better to drop an expensive computer. Mrs. Pierce is gonna kill me!"

An empty chair stood on the other side of the tree, and Sera dragged it over to sit and help collect the destroyed book's remains. "What was this anyway?" she asked, turning over the yellowed pages to get a look.

"It's called—it *was* called—*The Rise and Fall and Rise of the Roman Empire.* I don't need to tell you how fascinating—"

Sera held up a hand to cut him off. "Yeah, you're right, you don't need to tell me. I can only imagine the magic you felt as you tore through its riveting pages."

"Quit being a smart aleck," he said with eyes narrowed. "It *was* riveting. Only you could think making guesses about junk that's smaller than an atom is more exciting than reading about evil emperors cutting people up and bathing in their blood."

She stared at him, blinking once in exaggerated disinterest.

"Hungry?" he asked with a sly grin.

She tried to grin back but nothing came. "I had another one today," she said.

"A moon-sized pimple?" he asked.

She punched him in the arm. "A Remnant, you jerk."

His face fell a bit. "Oh. Sorry. I know those are hard on you."

"Sometimes I think they're getting worse. It's so hard to explain. But it hurts like nothing else."

"Weird."

Sera had been called weird before, and not always nicely. But she knew Dak meant it in a completely different way. And he was right. "Yeah, it *is* weird."

Dak gave up on the pile of paper and leather and shoved it all under the chair. Then he stood up. "I've got something that'll cheer you to pieces in a heartbeat."

"You do, huh?"

"I do." He pulled something out of his pocket. "My mom and dad left the keys to the lab out."

Sera had never heard such beautiful words in all her life. She didn't even bother responding—she was already on her feet and sprinting toward the back of the house.

The lab was a separate building in the back corner of the Smyths' property—a three-story brick structure with no windows and a single door made of black iron and sealed shut with about 197 locks by the look of it. When Dak had said that his parents left the keys out, he'd skipped the mundane details—that the keys were *usually* in a sealed box that was kept in a fireproof safe within a huge wall-sized gun locker. Sera thought it was all a little OCD—but Dak's parents had always been a bit odd.

Sera got there first, waiting impatiently in front of the

imposing door as Dak approached, jangling the keys in his hand. "It looks like something out of the Dark Ages, doesn't it?" he asked.

"How in the world did they forget to put the keys away?" Sera asked. "I'd expect them to catch their flight to Europe completely naked before letting something like that happen." Dak's parents went overseas at least once a month for some kind of business venture that no one had ever fully explained to Sera. It was how they made money to support their *real* passion—the oddball experiments and silly research projects rumored to be taking place inside the lab. Sera couldn't wait to check them out.

"Let's just say I helped them along a little," Dak answered. "I've been dying to see what they've been up to in here. Dad keeps saying they've come up with something really big. Really, really big. Maybe they finally came up with a working model of that regurgitating refrigerator he's always talked about."

Sera summed it up in a deadpan voice: "And so you stole their keys so that you can explore their inner sanctum completely against their will."

"I won't break anything if you don't."

"Pinkie swear?"

"Pinkie swear."

They hooked their little fingers and that was that. Dak's grandma was half blind and three-quarters deaf, so she'd never know they were up to something.

Dak flipped through the keys and started matching big ones and little ones with a series of locks that lined the right side of the door. Sera looked on as he worked, trying to hide the impatience that threatened to explode out of her. Here she had the chance of a lifetime to peruse a fully functioning science lab—no matter how silly the things that might be going on within.

Dak was on his knees now, trying to find the key to fit a lock that was only an inch above the ground.

"Is it your goal in life to drive me crazy?" Sera asked. "One more minute passes and I'm going to start ninja chopping your skinny head."

"You're awfully loud for a ninja," he said just as something clicked. "Got it!" The heavy door swung inward with a metallic scrape across the cement floor. Sera slipped past him and went inside before he could even stand up.

"Hurry and close it," she whispered to him, as if someone were listening in. She couldn't shake the feeling of being watched. The thought chilled her spine as Dak slammed the door closed.

There was a bank of switches to her right and she flipped them all, then watched in anticipation as lights flickered on one at a time, revealing the beauty of the lab in slow motion. It was huge, filled with everything she'd ever imagined would be in such a place—computers running along the walls, monitors atop every desk, and a jumble of electronics and chemicals and glassware on every available surface. Freestanding whiteboards were covered with a rainbow scrawl of mathematical and chemical formulas. The whole humongous room was a haven of science. It was far beyond what she'd expected from the Smyths.

Something to the left caught Sera's attention. She walked over to see a glass case, about the size and shape of a small refrigerator. Behind the glass, on a felt stand, there was a silvery band of metal an inch thick, shaped like a figure eight and about a foot long. Except for a small touch screen on one side, the object appeared completely smooth and shiny, almost shimmering like liquid. It looked alien—and very advanced.

"That must be it," Dak whispered. She didn't know when he'd appeared at her shoulder. "Their really, really big project. What in the world is it?"

There was a small label affixed to the glass case, three words that made Sera's heart skip a few beats.

The Infinity Ring.

Sera shifted her gaze to the right. Next to the display case, a whiteboard stood over a large desk on which several SQuares rested. Three more words were written across the top of the board—*The Missing Piece*—and a series of formulas had been laid out below them. Sera scanned the scrawl of letters and numbers and symbols, her fascination growing, and something tickled in her brain again. This time, she knew, it had nothing to do with a Remnant.

"Dak?" she said.

"Yeah?" He'd already wandered off.

"I'm going to need some time to myself. Your parents left behind quite a puzzle." She turned her head to look at him. "I want to know exactly what this is."

Hitting the SQuares

AFTER AN hour of wandering his parents' lab, Dak had had enough. Sera hadn't moved from the desk next to the Infinity Ring — whatever *that* meant — where she pored over his parents' notes and formulas. Dak wanted no part of that, figuring she'd find out some cool stuff then tell him about it later in terms he could understand. So he fiddled around, peeking at diagrams and models of things he couldn't name, jars full of gross stuff he couldn't identify, and books that seemed interesting at first glance but proved to be incomprehensible.

Sera didn't speak the entire time. Every once in a while a grunt or an "Ah!" would escape her, but nothing else. She was onto something, and when that happened, Dak knew he might as well leave her to it.

"Hey," he said to her. "I'm going to fix something to eat. Want anything?"

She didn't respond, didn't even look back at him. Instead she moved from one SQuare to another, flicking on its glowing display and leaning closer to read.

"Hey," he said again. "I'm gonna go down to Mrs.

Jackson's place and murder her whole family. Then I'm gonna fly to the moon and eat some chickens. Be right back."

"Okay," she murmured.

Man, is she onto something, he thought as he went out the door.

Several hours later, stuffing his face with potato chips, Dak still hadn't heard or seen from Sera. He was sitting on the couch flipping the TV back and forth between a fluff piece about the upcoming French royal wedding and news reports about twin hurricanes in the Gulf of Mexico, both category fives and too unpredictable to project where they might make landfall. Such things had grown almost tiresome to track, but there wasn't anything else to do.

He knew Sera would work until she died of starvation if left to her own devices, so he whipped up a couple of ham sandwiches and took them out to her. She accepted the plate without so much as a thank-you and started wolfing the food down, her eyes still on the SQuare in front of her.

"The moon was awesome," Dak said. "The chickens, too."

"Uh-huh," Sera said under her breath.

Hating what a waste the day had become, Dak slouched back to the house, wondering why he'd ever thought it a good idea to let Sera loose in such a place.

The shrill ring of the phone woke him up.

With groggy eyes, his mouth feeling like someone had stuffed a dirty sock in there, he looked over at the clock. In a panic, he shot to his feet. It was almost ten P.M.

Shrieking curses at no one in particular, he ran to the phone and answered it. Just as he expected, Sera's uncle was ranting and raving on the other end, wondering where she was—it was nearly curfew, and officers could pop in for a random check any minute. Dak apologized profusely, saying he'd get her right away. He thought Sera knew better than to risk being out past ten. Plus, her uncle had a really annoying nasally voice when he was ticked off.

"Sera!" Dak yelled when he burst through the iron door—as much as he *could* burst through it when the thing weighed more than the limestone blocks used to construct the Great Pyramid of Giza. "Do you have any clue what time it is? Your uncle's having a hissy fit! He says he won't cover for you if the SQ come around asking why you're out past curfew."

She didn't panic like he thought she would. Instead, she slowly stood up and turned to him. Somehow her face looked both exhausted and full of energy.

Dak almost wanted to take a step back. "Um . . . you okay, there?"

"The Infinity Ring is a time-travel device," she said, as calm as he'd ever seen her. "And I figured out the missing piece. I know how to make it work."

8

The Missing Piece

TIME TRAVEL. Dak didn't know which was cooler: The idea that such a thing was possible, or the fact that his parents might have been the ones to figure it out. Although he didn't know if he quite believed it, he couldn't help being excited at the very idea.

He spent almost every minute of Sunday with Sera, and he only understood about twenty percent of what came out of her mouth. She was working in the lab, reprogramming the Infinity Ring as he sat and watched. Making it even more annoying, she started half of her sentences with phrases like, "It's really simple if you think about it" or "Obviously" or "As you well know . . ."

And the *words* she used! "Space-time" and "relativity" and "cosmic strings" and "tachyons" and "quantum this" and "quantum that." Dak had a splintering headache by noon and no amount of medicine would make it go away.

Adding insult to injury, Dak was anxious that Sera's uncle might be knocking on their door at any second. It turned out the authorities *had* stopped in for a random check at Sera's house the night before, and they'd written her up for the violation. She'd been scolded by her terrified uncle and grounded, but that didn't stop *her*. No siree. She promised to stay in her room all day and read but instead she climbed out the window and ran to Dak's house before he'd even had a chance to take advantage of his parents' absence to eat a plate of cheese for breakfast.

And that still wasn't the worst of it. Dak was all too aware he'd broken more of his mom and dad's rules in one weekend than he had his entire life before that. And somehow he'd let Sera talk him into the ultimate sin against them.

She'd taken their most prized possession—ranking just slightly above Dak, no doubt—out of its protective glass case and had been playing with it for hours. She was messing around with a thing that probably had cost every spare penny they'd ever earned and could end up being the most valuable invention of all time. He winced every time she took a screwdriver to it. He nearly fainted when she used the soldering iron. He'd either believed her speeches about what she could do or he was the single stupidest person who'd ever lived. Either way, if this didn't work, he was going to be grounded for the next three thousand years.

It was just past five o'clock, all of these thoughts going through Dak's head on loop, when Sera put the device down on the desk and said one word:

"Done."

Dak blinked a few times. "What do you mean, *done*? That's the simplest word you've said all day, but it can't possibly mean what I think it means."

"I'm done, Dak." She pointed at the Ring. "That little thing right there will warp space-time and take a person into the past. I'm not sure why I should make it any more complicated than that."

Dak was finding her conclusion absolutely impossible to believe. He walked over and picked up the device. It was heavier than it looked, and cold to the touch. For the first time, Dak noticed a pencil-thin window that ran along the device's entire length. Behind the window was an amber-colored liquid. Fuel of some kind, he guessed.

"It wasn't even that hard," Sera said. There was no hint of bragging in her voice. It wasn't some lame attempt to fish for compliments. To her, it was just plain true.

Dak looked up at her. "So let me get this straight. My parents, who have PhDs from Amancio University and SQIT, have been working on this device for twenty years, and you figured it all out in a couple of days?"

Sera shrugged. "They helped. A little."

Dak threw up his arms.

"Hey, careful with that!" Sera snapped. She snatched it away from him. "For the love of mincemeat. I'm just kidding, and you know it. They did most of the work—ninety-nine-point-nine percent of it. Maybe they just needed someone with fresh eyes to come in and seal the deal. Figure out the missing piece of the puzzle. Like I said, it was—"

"Yeah, I know," Dak interrupted. "Easy. Piece of cake. Like . . . naming the presidents in order of how old they were when they got elected. Kid's stuff. But how do you know for sure that it *does* work?"

"Because all the formulas are balanced. The mechanics of it make sense now. I'd go into more detail, but based on how *riveted* you were by my earlier explanations, I think I'll spare you the pain. But I know it works. The same way you know that two plus two is four."

"Thanks for keeping it at my level. Anyway, what do we do now, genius?"

A huge smile lit up her face. "We tell your parents all about it."

He suddenly wanted to throw up and run to China.

Dak's parents were due home around seven o'clock that evening. His grandma figured he was a big boy and could take care of himself between dinner and their arrival, so she packed up, gave him a creaky hug, and went home. Dak loved her to death, but she had barely moved out of her chair in the guest room since showing up, so he wasn't quite sure why she was there in the first place. In case he needed a knitted sweater out of the blue?

The last half hour waiting for his mom and dad to

walk through the front door was agonizing. He and Sera sat on the couch in the living room, the *tick tick tick* of the clock on the wall the only sound.

Dak's hands were slick with sweat. There just wasn't any way that this could go down without getting ugly. He tried to think about how he'd break the news, and nothing sounded right. Not a single historical anecdote seemed appropriate to soften the blow. Taking the keys alone was enough to make his dad turn beet red and get his mom shrieking like a diseased monkey.

Three minutes after seven the door opened.

His mom stepped inside, holding a small suitcase in one hand and a giant purse in the other. His dad followed with the rest of their luggage. He shut the door with an elbow, then both of them noticed Dak and Sera sitting before them in silence.

"Well howdy do!" his dad said, a little too loudly. Dak didn't think anyone would ever need to know anything else about his father except that the man often said the words *Well howdy do!* That pretty much said it all.

"What are you two little munchkins up to?" his mom asked as she put her things down. "How nice of you to greet us—our own private welcoming committee! Where's the band and the cocktails?" She snorted a laugh, something that sounded like a pig getting tickled.

And these two people were geniuses. *Well*, Dak thought, *gotta love 'em.*

"Now where are my hugs?" his mom said with a mock hurt face. "Don't just sit there all day like two bumps on a pickle! Come over here."

Dak stood up . . . and suddenly had an idea. There was only one way to tell this story and survive to see the next day: backward.

"Mom, Dad," he said, hoping to make it clear that he had something serious to tell them.

Both of them had made it about halfway into the living room, but now they stopped and stared. They'd sensed it all right.

Dak smiled, trying to show what good news he had. "The Infinity Ring works now. She's all ready to go."

Dak's mom and dad both had confused looks on their faces, as if they mostly thought he was kidding but weren't completely sure.

"Come again?" his mom finally asked.

Dak stuck with telling the story backward — he wanted to leave that little tidbit about him stealing their keys until the very end. "It took all weekend, but Sera was able to fill in your missing piece, and now it works."

Sera was fidgeting beside him, still on the couch, her knees bouncing. His parents shared a look that he couldn't quite read.

Dak decided to keep going, thinking this just might work without an explosion of rage, groundings, unnecessary murders, stuff like that. "Look, we can fill in all the details later — but this is exciting, right? We need to get out there! Sera can explain, but the Infinity Ring is ready to be tested!"

"Who else knows about this?" Dak's mom said. Her voice was flat and commanding — it actually scared Dak a little.

"What . . . what do you mean?" he asked. Sera stood beside him now, and he could tell she sensed the bad shift in the mood.

Dak's mother put her hands on his shoulders. "This is important, son. Did you tell anyone what you were up to? Anyone at all? Your grandmother, maybe? Sera's uncle?"

"No," Dak said. He looked over at Sera, who shook her head. "Mom, what's going on?"

Dak's dad drew the curtains closed, his face pinched with worry. "This isn't a *game*, Dak. What on *earth* were you thinking?"

He yelled that last bit, something Dak had never, not once, experienced before.

"I'm sorry, Dad. But . . . we figured it out."

"You also might've signed our death warrants," his mom replied.

"We can't waste another second," his dad said. "Show us."

9

The Breathless Wait

THE NEXT couple of hours were a complete nightmare. First, Dak had to sit through Sera's explanations on how everything worked and how she'd figured it out. His parents were short and bitter as they asked questions and demanded answers. Then Sera's uncle came over and caused a major scene when he started screaming and yelling. Somehow Dak's dad was able to calm the old geezer down, convince him that Sera desperately needed their help with an important homework project, and send him on his way.

Then there was another hour of scientific mumbo jumbo that just about drove Dak over the edge. Just when he thought he couldn't take any more, he heard someone say his name. His head jerked up and he realized he'd been staring at the floor.

His dad was standing right in front of him, arms folded across his chest. "Maybe you should try listening harder—you might learn something."

"Science isn't my thing, Dad." They'd had this

conversation a million times. The truth was that Dak did well enough in the subject at school, but it just didn't interest him. And they were talking about things well beyond anything he'd learned in school anyway. "But I'd be happy to tell you about the political implications after pyroglycerine was developed by Italy in 1847."

Sera and his mom were still bent over a SQuare, gesticulating and talking in an excited rush. His mom had the Ring gripped in her left hand. Dak returned his attention to his dad, whose stern expression made his face look like hard stone. Both of his parents looked older than ever before, like they'd aged twenty years in a matter of days.

And then the lecture began. "I don't think I need to tell you how disappointed I am that you broke some of our most sacred rules. A lot of bad things could've happened. Not just to our research, but to you. Quantum mechanics is *not* something to be messed with. Not to even mention the fact that certain parties wouldn't be very happy to learn about what we've been up to here. Do you understand why we're so upset?"

"Yes, sir." Dak showed a sad face but on the inside he was leaping with joy — this was the lamest, shortest discipline speech he'd ever gotten. "I'm sorry."

His dad smiled. "I think she did it, Dak. I think this thing will really work."

"You're serious?" Dak was pretty sure he should be more excited about the time-travel device than his escape from punishment, but at the moment it was a tie.

"Dead serious." Dak's dad looked over his shoulder at his wife and Sera, then back at Dak. "We'll try to act like all is normal until tomorrow afternoon, throw the scent off if there is one. Then your mom and I are going to do a test run. For your sake, Dak, I hope the SQ somehow missed your shenanigans."

Dak had experienced some long days at school before. But this one was ridiculous. Knowing that when he got home, he was going to witness something momentous sort of put a damper on the usual school-day fare.

It was nearly four thirty when Dak, Sera, and Dak's parents were finally gathered in the laboratory, sitting around a table, facing one another with grim looks that didn't completely hide their excitement. Dak had always thought of his parents as a little bit on the goofy side, but they were all business now.

"Okay," Dak's mom said, leaning forward on her elbows. "You kids ready for this?" Evidently she included her husband in the subject of that question. When all three nodded, she continued. "Good. The plan is this: The two of us are going to take a very brief trip, then come right back here. We'd like you two to stay in the lab in case . . . well, to make sure everything goes as planned."

"You're *both* going?" asked Dak. "With a single Ring?"

Dak's dad answered with a stiff nod. "The device works by warping the fabric of space-time to create a wormhole—basically a tunnel that leads from wherever you're standing to wherever you've programmed the device to take you. But it doesn't just transport the person who's holding the Ring. In addition to the pilot, any person that the pilot is touching will get pulled along for the ride."

"And so will inanimate objects," his mom added. "Though there are limits as to how much mass we can take with us. If I were to use the Ring in a car, the car wouldn't travel back in time with me. But the seat belt I was wearing might. Got it?"

"Got it," Dak and Sera said in unison.

"We'd bring you a souvenir, honey, but we can't interfere with the past," his mom said. "Even stepping on a bug could have ripple effects that drastically alter the future. I mean, the present." She gave a little snort-chuckle then, for the first time since she'd learned the Ring was operational.

Oddly enough, it wasn't until then that the reality began to sink in for Dak. The idea itself had seemed so cool, but now it hit him hard and heavy. Panic flared inside him. What if his parents blinked out of existence and never came back? He couldn't imagine letting them go, then being left to wonder what had happened to them.

They apparently didn't share his concerns.

Dak's mom stood up. "Okay. Let's quit talking and let's get warping."

1 0

The Infinity Ring

EVERYONE JOINED Dak's mom at the glass case, where she carefully pulled out the Infinity Ring and held the shiny silver loop in her hands like a strange steering wheel. "Your dad and I decided last night that we want to protect this investment from being stolen and used by others. We can do that by keying the device to our DNA. No one else will ever be able to use it. Other Rings can be built when and if we share the technology, but this prototype is our family's and no one else's. Sera, we're including you because of your obvious and amazing contributions."

"Me?" Sera said. "You want me to do it, too?"

"Of course," Dak's mom answered. "I know we've been harsh, but it's only because we care about you both. We want you to feel included, and if everything goes smoothly today, we may bring you two along on a later voyage. We might even need you to control the device if we've got our hands full."

Sera nodded. Dak had never seen her look so proud before.

One by one, they each pricked their thumb on a sterile medical device that plugged right into a port on the side of the Ring. Then Dak's mom and dad each took a turn doing some programming, conferring with each other to make sure everything was absolutely correct. And then it was time.

"The Ring is programmed with the appropriate coordinates," Dak's dad said. "We're planning on spending a few minutes at our destination. But the beauty of time travel is that theoretically we can be back here just a split second after we leave."

"Theoretically?" repeated Dak.

"So for us, this trip will last a few minutes," said Dak's mom. "But from your perspective, we'll be back in the blink of an eye."

"Now step back, kids," said her husband. "And cross your fingers."

Dak looked on anxiously as his mom pushed a small button on the Infinity Ring. A hum filled the room, like a hive of bees had just awakened. There was a tingly vibration in the air, as if someone had just dinged a thousand tuning forks.

The dark amber liquid within the Ring glowed bright orange, filling the lab with light.

Dak suddenly couldn't take it anymore. "We're going, too!" He grabbed Sera by the hand and reached out to grip his father's elbow.

He barely had time to see his parents' shocked faces before everything around them exploded into a tube of light and sound that sucked the lab away and threw their bodies into a chaotic spin. Flashes of alternating color and darkness flew past him but he couldn't keep his eyes open long enough to see any detail. His ears popped and his tongue swelled and his stomach rolled and the world seemed to press in on him. He tried to scream but the awful noise was so loud he couldn't even tell if he'd done it. Pinpricks of pain broke out all over him, *inside* him, as if he were beginning to crack like an eggshell, about to burst into a million pieces at any second.

And then, just as quickly as it had started, it ended.

Dak found himself standing on a flattened patch of grass under a sunny blue sky. His parents and Sera were right next to him, all three of them looking at him with fire in their eyes.

He quickly dropped Sera's hand.

"I'm sorry!" Dak blurted. "I couldn't stand the thought of waiting around, wondering what happened to you guys."

Dak's dad pointed a finger at him. "You have no idea what you've—"

A roar behind them cut off his words. Dak spun around to see the source—about a hundred yards away, scores of soldiers dressed in red coats and white pants came running over the crest of a hill. Each one of them held a long rifle with a blade attached to the end. Dak was suddenly in his element, and the coolness of what he saw before him overwhelmed any sense of fear or guilt.

These were British soldiers, and those blades on the end of their guns were called bayonets. The muskets they carried weren't like modern-day weapons that could shoot bullet after bullet in rapid succession. It took a lot longer to shoot just one bullet — or ball — with the guns that were pointed at them now. That was why they had the bayonets, so the soldiers could fight like sword-wielding knights when it came to that.

"No way!" Dak said. "You guys were going to visit the Revolutionary War without me?"

"This isn't a game!" Dak's dad shouted.

"We have a hundred men charging in to kill us," his mom said rather calmly.

Dak had to admit that the bayonets seemed slightly less cool the closer they got.

Sera pointed at a copse of trees about thirty yards away, out of the direct path of the small army. "Let's run over there. They're obviously not after us, because they didn't know we existed thirty seconds ago. We just happened to land in their path."

Dak knew she was right. She was logical like that. "Good thinking."

The four of them ran to the spot she'd indicated and slipped through the outer layer of trees to crouch behind some bushes. The soldiers had surely seen them, but Dak hoped they wouldn't worry about a stray family — albeit a stray family in strange clothing.

The army had come into full view now, running down the slope to the area where Dak and the others had appeared out of nowhere. When they reached that spot, the soldiers were ordered to halt by a commanding officer. Then, without any kind of instruction, they lined up in three perfectly straight rows, still facing the direction in which they'd been heading.

"I need to fine-tune some of the satellite grid inputs," Dak's dad whispered. "Everything dealing with location is based on how things are mapped out in the future by the GPS system, but it's not quite accurate enough. And we obviously don't have the satellites now. We were supposed to be about a mile from here so we could watch this from a safe distance."

"Where are we?" Sera asked. "And . . . *when* are we?"

Dak jumped all over that. "We're smack-dab in the middle of the Revolutionary War. Those are British soldiers and they're obviously expecting a battle with some American militiamen. Keep watching and you'll see how organized and rigid the British are, and how wild and crazy the Americans are. I can't believe I'm seeing this!"

His mom shushed him. "Quiet down!"

Dak felt an almost unbearable thrill of excitement as it finally hit him what was going on. They'd just traveled through time! He'd just leapt back hundreds of years using a device dreamed up by his own parents and perfected by his best friend. Judging by the half-glazed look on Sera's face, she was coming to the same world-altering realization.

Movement out in the ranks grabbed his attention. Three red-coated soldiers were running toward them, guns raised.

"You there!" one of them shouted. "American spies!

Come out or we'll shoot!" He and his partners kept coming at full speed.

"*That's* not good," Dak said. "Do you know what they did to American spies? Because I do, and—"

Sera silenced him with a glance.

"What do we do?" Dak's mom asked.

"Don't worry," her husband answered with forced calm. He was pressing buttons on the Infinity Ring. "Keep your heads down. I'm almost there."

One of the soldiers fired a shot, smoke and fire flashing from the muzzle of his weapon. The ball smashed into a tree right next to Dak's head.

"Almost there!" his dad repeated.

But it was too late. The soldiers crashed into the trees, throwing their weapons down and grabbing at the visitors from the future. The biggest redcoat pulled Sera by the shirt, ripping her off her feet. Dak moved in to help her but the man swung a fist, slamming it into Dak's cheek. He fell to the ground, dazed. The other two soldiers tussled with his parents, pushing at them roughly. Dak caught a glimpse of his dad, struggling to hide the Infinity Ring and work on it at the same time as he was being roughed up.

Dak's mom tore loose and fell on Dak, pulling him into her arms. Sera ripped herself free at the same time and jumped toward them. They huddled as a group and backed into his dad, who still fidgeted with the device.

There was a humming sound. The trees around them started to shake. Dak saw one of the soldiers pick up a gun he'd dropped. The bayonet on the end glinted in the sunlight, breaking through the branches above them. He lifted the gun like a spear and charged at their small group. Sera's arms came up as if she could actually deflect the vicious blade.

Everything around them turned into chaos and color and sound.

Dak, his parents, Sera—all of them were ripped from the copse of trees, sucked into a wormhole. In that blur of movement and noise, Dak felt as if his body were frozen, but the others seemed to be moving. Dak's mom had let go and turned to hug her husband, and the two of them looked as if they were dancing, the edges of their skin tendriling out like streams of their soul being torn away.

Someone squeezed Dak's hand—he forced his head to move as if through a thick liquid or a tremendous wind, and he saw Sera looking at him. Still they flew through the wormhole, the rush of noise almost deafening.

An object was in Dak's other hand. He knew it by touch: the Infinity Ring. When had his father given it to him? He didn't have time to think, just gripped it in his fingers. The lights grew brighter, the sound impossibly louder. Dak screamed but the sound of it was lost in the madness.

Then it all ended. Dak and Sera appeared on the floor of the lab.

There was no sign of his parents. Anywhere.

11

Black Hoods and Black Cars

SERA COULDN'T quite process what was wrong at first. She'd just had the craziest ten minutes of her entire life, and now she stood back in the quiet lab of Mr. and Mrs. Smyth. Her mind felt a little bent, as if it had just gone up in an airplane and done loops. Parts of her body were hot and other parts were cold. Dak stood next to her, staring at something in his hands. She followed his gaze and saw that he clutched the Infinity Ring.

The soldiers were nowhere to be seen — but neither were Dak's parents.

He was frozen, his eyes glued to the Ring.

"Dak," Sera whispered.

His free hand shot up, palm toward her, telling her to be quiet.

She let a few seconds pass but couldn't stand it anymore. "Dak, what do—"

"Be quiet!" he yelled. "They're going to show up any second now."

Sera felt a painful thumping in her chest, a mix of panic and aching hurt for Dak. Something terrible had happened, and she wasn't sure why. But if his parents hadn't appeared yet, they weren't going to appear at all.

"Dak, listen to me. . . ."

He turned toward her, his face at first full of fire and anger. But it quickly melted into despair. His lips trembled.

"What happened?" he asked, his voice cracking. "Where are they?"

"I don't know." In that moment she felt responsible—had she messed something up in her calculations? "I'm sorry." She hated that her words sounded so empty.

Dak turned on her, thrusting the Infinity Ring into her hands. "Fix this! Help them! Do something!"

"Dak, we'll figure this out, but you need to calm down," she said.

"Easy for you to say! You have no idea . . ." He started pacing around the room, looking as if he wanted something to kick.

But before he found anything there was a sudden explosion behind them.

Sera screamed and fell to the floor, instinctively turning her body to avoid landing on the Ring. Lights danced before her eyes as the huge iron door jumped a couple of feet forward then fell down, its ringing *boom* shaking the entire building.

Then came the people. They stormed into the lab in the wake of the tremendous crash—people dressed head to toe in black. At least a dozen of them.

Oh, no, thought Sera. *It's the SQ.*

Dak freaked out, punching wildly at the intruders as Sera scrambled to her feet. She was shocked and confused and suddenly terrified that these people were going to put a bullet in Dak's brain.

"Dak! Stop it!" she shouted, but he seemed like he'd lost his mind. Several men tackled him to the ground, subduing him roughly.

Sera didn't know what to do. Her only thought was that she could use the Infinity Ring to get them out of there, but she'd barely had the idea before people were grabbing her, taking the Ring out of her hands. She kicked and flailed to no avail, screaming at the black-clothed thugs.

"Both of you calm down!" someone yelled at them. "We're doing this for your own good!"

But Sera and Dak didn't stop fighting as the intruders dragged them through the door and away from the laboratory.

They finally stopped thrashing once they were locked in the backseat of a car and black hoods were pulled over their heads. Sera fumbled for the door handle, but it was locked tight. It took a while for the two of them to calm their breathing, but silence eventually fell over them as the vehicle drove for miles and miles.

Dak didn't make a peep as they rocketed through endless unseen streets. But every once in a while his shoulder trembled, and she knew he was stifling a sob. She wished she could talk to him, tell him that she knew all too well what it was like to have missing parents. Even though she'd never met her own, the pain was like a hole in her heart. But she couldn't find the words.

If she couldn't cheer him up, she could at least try to keep him safe. She resolved to do whatever it took to get him out of this mess.

On they went, turn after turn, the car silent, the mood gloomy.

What light Sera could see through the coarse fabric of the hood suddenly cut out when the car pitched downward then upright again, as if they'd gone under- ground or into the lower floor of a garage. There was a bang of metal and the vehicle bounced before speeding forward again.

Soon they came to a stop. Someone escorted them out of the car and led them forward, steering Sera by her elbow. Although Sera couldn't see where they were going, she kept her ears trained on Dak's shuf- fling footsteps. There didn't seem to be much point in fighting, but if they dared to separate her from Dak, she would try.

Their captors didn't take the hood off her until they'd reached a metal door. Sera quickly looked around. They were in a dark garage, just as she'd guessed, but only a few cars were parked there. It seemed to have been carved out of rock, with uneven walls and ceiling. Dak wouldn't look her in the eyes. A blond man had them each by the arm, and he nodded toward the silvery door.

"Down the elevator we go," he said. "Then all of your questions will be answered."

Down the elevator they went.

Three floors down. A long hallway. A right turn, a left turn, and a second left. Another long hallway. Sera thought she'd keep track in case they had the chance to make an escape, but wherever they were, the place was built like a labyrinth.

And then, finally, they reached a small room with a table and four chairs. Two of those were occupied, by a man and a woman. They were both about the age of Dak's parents. The man looked a little goofy—big nose, black hair sticking up—but the woman was stunningly beautiful, with dark skin and a flawless face. Sera wished Dak was in the mood to make one of his famously awkward historical speeches in an attempt to break the ice. It might bore everyone else, but right now it would lift her spirits. Dak remained silent, though. His face was sallow and droopy, and his eyes were red and moist.

On the table was a spread of food that looked too good to be true. Fruit and cheese and cakes and pastries. Sera's stomach rumbled with hunger. The traitor.

The blond guard motioned for Dak and Sera to take the two empty chairs. Then, to their enormous surprise, he handed the Infinity Ring to Dak. "We'll be right outside if you need us," the guard said to the woman. She simply nodded.

The door closed behind him, and a weighty silence settled on the room. Dak clutched the Infinity Ring to his chest.

The man spoke first. "Well. Dak and Sera. We have so much to say to you. It's hard to even know where to start."

"Don't you think we should start by telling them our *names*?" the woman asked, giving her partner a reproving glare.

"Oh, yes, of course we should." The man cleared his throat. "My name is Brint, and this is my colleague, Mari. We, um, both know who you are. Although I guess you've figured that out by now. Please feel free to help yourselves to some food. If there's anything else you want—"

Sera had reached the end of her rope. "We had a fridge full of food back at Dak's house. You know, where we were when your goons trespassed on private property, set off explosives, and *kidnapped* us? We're not in very good moods, and what we *want* is to know what's going on!"

Brint had flinched at Sera's outburst, leaning back as far as he could in his chair, a look of complete shock on his face. Mari hadn't moved a muscle.

"Well?" Sera pushed.

"I like your spirit," Mari said quietly. "You're going to need it for what we're about to ask of you. But rein in the outbursts and Brint will tell you everything you need to know. Brint?"

Sera watched as the man shifted in his seat uncomfortably. It was obvious who was really in charge here. But Brint quickly recovered and took on a serious air as he leaned forward and folded his hands on the table.

"We're members of a group called the Hystorians," he began. "You wouldn't have heard of us, but our organization goes back many, many centuries. It was founded by the great philosopher Aristotle in 336 BC. We've lasted in a continuous line ever since, united in a common goal to one day save the world from a disaster that only a visionary like Aristotle could have predicted. And today you've given us the biggest breakthrough since he spoke of that vision. Time travel."

Sera glanced over at Dak, who sat up a little straighter, eyes focused on Brint. She was sure he felt the same relief she did — they hadn't been taken by the SQ after all. *If* these people weren't lying.

"Time travel?" Dak asked. "What does that have to do with Aristotle?"

Brint tightened his lips and nodded. "It has everything to do with him. He knew time travel would be possible someday, and he knew what it would be needed for. To go back and correct the Great Breaks. To remove the Remnants that haunt us. To set right the world's course and prevent reality from ending in a fiery Cataclysm."

The man paused and gave a long look to Sera, then Dak. "History is broken, and we need your help to fix it."

12

The Hystorians

THERE WAS an emptiness inside Dak unlike anything he'd ever experienced. The shock and anger of losing his parents had worn off, leaving a numbness that was somehow worse. Numbness, and confusion. He had no idea what had happened, which wasn't entirely surprising. The bad news was that Sera didn't seem to know either. All he could say for sure was that they were gone, and the ache was like a choking smoke in his lungs.

But Brint's words had pierced through the haze. Dak felt a spark of something. It wasn't quite enough to make him forget his misery. But it was enough to get him interested.

"What does that *mean*?" Dak asked. "Fix history?"

"The world is not *right*, Dak, Sera. It's gone off the rails, and we needed time travel to get it back on course."

"But . . ." Sera began. "But history's, well, *history*, isn't it?"

"Let me start from the beginning," Brint suggested. "We don't have a lot of time—pardon the irony—but you two need to have a general understanding of what we're dealing with. Are you ready for the story?"

Sera gave Dak a look that told him she was worried that he was going to fall apart at any second. And he probably *would* fall apart if he got any sympathy right now. So he put on a dopey grin and rubbed his hands together.

"I'm always ready for a story that starts with Aristotle," he said.

Brint smiled. "Aristotle is my personal hero. He was one of the greatest minds of his time or any before it. As such, he was chosen at the age of forty-one by the king of Macedon, King Philip II, to become the tutor of his son, Alexander. Aristotle felt in his heart that Alexander would go on to do great things. He felt this very, very strongly—he even called the boy Alexander the Great so that he'd be aware of what was expected of him. But it all went wrong.

"In 336 BC, Alexander and his father were assassinated by a man named Attalas, the king's own father-in-law, so that the grandson of Attalas could be the next king instead of Alexander. That boy was Karanos, Alexander's half brother, and he did indeed become the next ruler, and went on to oversee a time of terrible darkness for Asia. Aristotle was devastated. He never really got over it."

Now Dak was truly fascinated. He knew this story, of course—he'd been on a major ancient Greece kick just a few years before—but he had no idea what it had to do with anything that was going on now. He listened intently as the man continued, almost managing to ignore the ache that still swelled within his chest.

"Aristotle had an understanding of the world and its workings that far surpassed anyone of his period. He believed the universe had an order to it, that there is a fabric of reality in which the stories of life are woven. And deep in his heart, he knew, absolutely knew, that Alexander was not supposed to have been murdered that day. Alexander's death represented a tear in the very fabric of reality. And, being the visionary man that he was, Aristotle planned to *make things right*."

"How?" Dak and Sera asked together.

Dak went further. "How did he plan on reversing a murder?"

Mari answered this time, tucking her hair behind an ear. "Time travel. He believed it was possible — not in his own era, but someday. He held out hope that mankind would develop the means to navigate the time stream. To go back and correct the things that didn't go the way they were supposed to go. Because if Alexander's fate had gone wrong, it seemed to him that other problems would likely arise as time marched on. He called these incidents Breaks, and Alexander the Great's murder was only the first."

"But people die every day!" Sera said. "And think about how many horrible things have happened throughout history. All the wars, all the abuse, all the suffering. How could we possibly go back and stop every tragedy?"

Mari was shaking her head before Sera had even

finished. "It's not like that. This isn't necessarily about *bad* things that have happened. For good or ill, most of history is part of the natural fabric of reality. We're talking about events that never should have happened to begin with."

"I don't buy it," Sera said.

"Sera . . ." Dak began.

"No! Dak, you're too trusting. I can understand that this Aristotle guy was torn up over his student getting killed. I totally get that he'd wish he could go back and change what had happened. But who is he to decide what was *supposed* to happen and what wasn't? How could he possibly know that?"

"Because of the Remnant," Brint answered. The cheeriness in his voice had disappeared entirely. He caught Sera's eyes. "Ah. I think you know what I mean. I think you've experienced a Remnant yourself, haven't you? They're unpleasant as a general rule. And Aristotle experienced the very first Remnant in history."

"That definitely wasn't in the biography I read," said Dak. "And it was a very long biography."

"It wouldn't have made any of the public records," Mari explained. "Aristotle had a traumatic vision at Alexander's funeral—a vision of the great man and leader that Alexander would have become. But he knew better than to speak of it—after all, Karanos was king now, and suggesting that he *shouldn't* be king would have been treason. So Aristotle only shared this knowledge with a small group of trusted friends and students. These were the first Hystorians, and they began a tradition that's stretched throughout centuries and across continents, documenting the subsequent Breaks. In effect, we've been recording an entire secret history."

"A secret history?" echoed Dak. "You mean there's *more* history to learn?"

Sera only rolled her eyes.

Brint cleared his throat. "And all of that leads us to the Cataclysm. More than a dozen Breaks have been officially listed as matching Aristotle's criteria. Everything from the kidnapping of a First Lady, to a botched mission in Europe during World War Two that had significant consequences. These Breaks not only led to undesirable outcomes, they severely damaged *reality itself.* The Remnants are one consequence of that. The increasingly intense natural disasters are another. Everything is falling apart, as you must be more than aware."

Dak thought about that — his knowledge of history left no doubt that the rate of earthquakes, tornadoes, hurricanes, and volcano eruptions had increased dramatically over the last hundred years. But to think that was somehow tied to certain events in history taking an unplanned route was . . . crazy. Just plain crazy.

"I can see those wheels spinning in your head," Brint said to him. "I know this all must seem unlikely. But I swear to you, with all my honor as a Hystorian — and I've devoted my life to this — that what we're telling you is true."

"It's a lot more complicated than we've laid it out,"

Mari added. "But this is the gist of it. Aristotle created a society that would diligently track and pass down records of the Great Breaks throughout the years, hoping that someday the Hystorians would pioneer time travel and go back to correct what went wrong. And that's where we stand today."

Brint tapped his finger on the table. "Of course, there's an even more immediate danger than earthquakes or Remnants."

Dak waited, wondering, *What now?*

"The SQ," Brint announced. "They've been around just as long as the Hystorians, though they've been known by many names. And where the rest of the world has suffered, they've actually benefited from the Breaks. As you might imagine, they're not thrilled with the idea that somebody might change that."

"What Brint is trying to say," Mari continued, "is that the SQ has eyes and ears everywhere. And if they were to catch wind of what we're up to here, they'd kill us all without hesitation."

"We can keep you safe," Brint said. "But only if you give us that Ring."

13

A Dangerous Turn

SERA DIDN'T like Brint's tone—she didn't like this turn in the conversation at all. She quickly squeezed Dak's hand before her friend could say anything. They had to play this right.

"I think the stakes are well-defined here," Brint continued. "We need that Ring so we can reverse engineer it. Make our own. And begin the process of fixing history." He and Mari looked squarely at Dak, who held the Ring clutched to his chest.

"Um," Dak started before Sera could stop him. "I don't know. All this stuff you're saying makes sense, I guess, but . . . *I* need the Ring. I have to find my mom and dad."

Sera knew Dak could be talked into anything—he was trusting to a fault. That meant it was up to her to protect their interests here, and she had no problem speaking up. "How did you people even know we *had* an operating time-travel device? Were you monitoring the area for stray chronon particles?"

Brint's eyes flickered to Mari's. "Um, yes, that's exactly how we knew what you were up to."

Sera scoffed at how easily she'd tricked them. "There's no such thing as a chronon! The Hystorians have been spying on the Smyths all along, haven't they? You're no better than the SQ!"

Brint stuttered and stammered. Mari cleared her throat, stepping in to take charge of the conversation. "Okay. Yes. We've been . . . monitoring Dak's parents. But we're not like the SQ, I promise you. We've only done what we have for the good of the world. How do you think the Smyths got the money they needed for their research, anyway? The Hystorians have been funding them all along, in secret, providing grants that they didn't know came from us."

"Which, by the way," Brint interjected, "gives us partial claim to the Ring technology."

Sera took a moment to consider her next move. Brint and Mari seemed genuine enough. But she didn't dare let the Ring out of her sight — not until Dak's parents were safe. And if Brint and Mari had been monitoring the lab, they knew that the Ring was all but useless without Sera's know-how . . . and without Dak or Sera to activate it. That was an advantage she could use.

"If you knew anything about this technology," she said, "you'd know that it would take months to make your own device. At least."

Brint and Mari exchanged a long, worried look. It was obvious they didn't have that kind of time.

"You need us," Dak blurted out, the excitement sparking in his eyes as he caught on to Sera's train of thought. "You need us to use our own device. We have to pilot the thing." He turned to Sera. "We can do this. We can do all of it at once! Find my parents. Save the world. Maybe even get rid of the Remnants."

For some reason, that hit her in the gut like a punch. Would not having a false memory of her parents be better? Or worse? She didn't even want to think about it.

But she could see that Brint and Mari knew that Dak was right. The Hystorians *did* need them. "We'll help you," she said, "but we'll only do it if you promise to help us find Dak's parents. Take it or leave it."

"You'll have to leave the dirty work to the adults," Brint said. He turned to Mari, waiting until she gave a reluctant nod before he continued. "While we devote resources here to figuring out what happened to Dak's parents, you can act as escorts for a crack team of Hystorians. Our people will do the actual work of fixing the Breaks, but their lives will depend on you two getting them where they need to be. And following their orders to the letter. There are the Time Wardens to worry about, after all."

"Time Wardens?" Dak repeated.

"When I said the SQ had eyes and ears everywhere, I didn't just mean in the present," Mari explained. "You see, if it weren't for the Breaks, the SQ might not hold all the power they do in the world today. Their Lady in Red may not be as omniscient, seeing all. So while we've been hoping all along for time travel to become a reality, the SQ has been dreading it. Just as we've sworn to someday go back and change the past, they've sworn not to let that happen. And they've had people trained in every generation to stop the mission we're about to undertake."

"There are people in the past specifically on the look-out for time travelers?" Sera asked. "That's crazy!"

"It's good strategy," Mari countered. "They're called Time Wardens. And if they ever even *suspect* that someone has come back from the future, they're instructed to kill them without blinking an eye."

Sera felt a shiver of fear at that. The room fell silent, as if Brint and Mari wanted to give everyone a moment to process the danger they would be in.

Dak broke the ice. "Fine. We'll leave the scary stuff to the adults. Now are you guys ever going to let us eat this food?"

"By all means," Mari replied, smiling as she pushed the platter toward Dak. "There's even some fine cheese hidden in there somewhere."

Dak and Sera dug in without saying another word. Mari seemed pleased with the outcome they'd agreed on, but Sera could feel anxious energy coming off of Brint. He was clearly ready to put them all to work.

"Let's walk to the operations center," he said after everyone else had enjoyed a quick helping of treats. "That is . . . if you're done eating?"

Dak whipped his hand out and grabbed one last cube of Swiss then stuffed it in his mouth. "Now I am," he mumbled while chewing.

As they walked down a long, dimly lit hallway, Mari gave them a few more details about what lay ahead. Sera listened eagerly.

"In addition to the trained members of our society that we'll send back with you," the woman said, "there's also a local Hystorian already living in the vicinity of most of the Breaks. We've had a steady membership of Hystorians since Aristotle's time, spread out in branches all over the world. Their locations are hidden, but every single one of us has always been trained to look for people from the future."

"Why can't they just fix the Breaks themselves?" Sera asked. "Or prevent them?"

Dak gave her a look that, even in the relative darkness, left no doubt she had said something ridiculous, and she quickly blurted out the answer to her own question before he could. "Oh, duh. Wasn't thinking. They don't know what a Break is until after it's happened."

"Exactly," Mari responded. "The Hystorians have always analyzed major events of the world, and, aided in part by the appearance of new Remnants, decided well after the fact if an event is an official Break or not. But they also know that someone may show up one day and tell them of an event that is *about* to take place. They're trained to prepare for that possibility. You're the pilots, mainly. Messengers. Remember that. The adults will be ready to do what needs to be done."

Dak bristled. "Hey, we're not moron wimps, ya know. We can help, too."

"I don't doubt that at all," Mari said as they came to a halt in front of a large steel door. She pulled something out of a leather satchel she had slung around her shoulder—a SQuare slate device—and held it up for them to see.

"All of the information you need will be downloaded to this," she said. "Don't worry—we've completely overwritten the SQ software, and there are so many firewalls built around this thing that it's more secure than your own brains. It will have all the information your team will need, although, again, it'll be encoded."

"It's all part of a system called The Art of Memory," Brint added. "Or TAM for short. It was actually devised by Aristotle so that data could be passed down from generation to generation without risking it falling into the hands of our enemies. Trust me when I tell you that it's gonna drive you bonkers sometimes. But you can do it."

"I'll bet I can do it with my eyes closed," said Dak.

"That doesn't even make any sense," said Sera.

Mari slipped the SQuare back into the satchel then gestured at the menacing door. "This is the HOC— Hystorian Operations Center. Are you two ready?"

Sera glanced over at Dak, who was actually smiling. *Smiling.* Maybe he'd survive his parents' disappearance after all. They both nodded at each other with knowing looks.

"We're ready," Sera said, right before Dak added his own confirmation:

"The Time Nerds are a go."

Lady in Red

MARI ACTIVATED a touch screen to the right of the door and input a long series of numbers and letters, a longer password than Dak had ever seen anyone use before. This Art of Memory thing seemed for real, and he found himself wishing he hadn't been so boastful about it. Now he had to live up to the expectation.

A *hiss* sounded, followed by a hollow, grating *scratch* as the metal bars of the lock pulled back. Then the door popped open and swung outward with a heavy groan.

"In we go," Mari said, holding an arm out to indicate the two kids should go first.

Dak gripped the cool surface of the Infinity Ring in his hand and stepped through the opening. Applause broke out and he saw at least twenty people standing up to clap from their various stations of computers and radar screens and monitors and other equipment. They all had hopeful smiles, and for the first time Dak felt the pressure of what they were being asked to do.

Save the world. No biggie, right?

Mari and Brint led them around a wide walkway that skirted the outside edge of the massive operations center. The central focal point was a monitor as big as a movie screen, but instead of displaying a single image it was broken up into dozens of views—everything from live video feed to running numbers to Doppler radar maps.

While Brint plugged the SQuare into a computer, Mari stepped up to a podium that overlooked the crew of workers at their stations. "I want everyone to meet our new Hystorians, granted membership without the usual years of proving ground. Urgent times call for urgent doings. This is Dak, and this is Sera."

Another round of applause met this statement, and Dak suddenly felt like the biggest idiot ever born. He'd just wanted to whip out the Ring and start touring history. Save the world and find his parents while he was at it. But here was an entire room full of people who were devoting their lives to a noble cause, hoping all along that someone would come along and give them the means to stop an unending series of tragedies.

Mari continued her speech. "We have a lot to do over the next couple of days before we send Dak, Sera, and our insertion squad back in time to fix the Breaks. Our current plan is to begin the operation at 0800 hours on Thursday. I know everyone's eager to begin, but we need two days to fully prep our new associates."

She went on to say more, but Dak tuned out. He was having a heavy episode of missing his parents, worrying about what could've happened to them. Two days was a long time to do nothing. And while he was here, they were out there somewhere—lost, possibly hurt, maybe running afoul of one of the Time Wardens. Finally, he understood a little about Sera's haunting Remnant. Loss, mixed with a maddening uncertainty.

He noticed Brint was looking at him expectantly.

"Um, oh, sorry," Dak stuttered. "Did I miss something?"

Brint smiled. "I asked if you were ready to start meeting people."

"Oh. Yeah. Sure."

And so they started making the rounds, but all the names and faces quickly became a jumble to Dak. Some dude who was in charge of tracking natural disasters and their frequency. Some chick who watched for anomalies in weather patterns. Some other dude who mapped out daily world events and analyzed them for potential Break material. Some other chick who tracked SQ activity overseas. Other dudes and other chicks who did other things.

Dak kept yawning even though he tried not to—which meant he kept doing that weird contorted face trick. Sera shot him dirty looks about every thirty seconds.

One Hystorian they met stood out from the pack. His name was Riq and he was far younger than everyone else, with dark skin and darker eyes. He was a kid compared to the rest of the geezers in the room.

"Riq is an absolute prodigy when it comes to languages," Brint said when he introduced him. "He learned five languages by the age of five, and he's set a goal to pick up one a year since then."

"You guys are supposed to be smart," the young man

said. "I'm sixteen. You've got three seconds to guess how many languages I know. Go."

"*Sixteen,*" Sera said, her voice laced with annoyance.

"Wow," Riq responded. "Stunning. No wonder they chose you for this."

"They didn't choose us," Dak said. "We invented a time-travel device and no one else can make it work. Ever done that before? Invent a time-travel device?"

Riq rattled off something in another language. All Dak knew was that it had a lot of clearing of the throat.

"You need to spit somewhere?" Dak asked him. "Or did you swallow part of your oversized brain?"

"If I did, maybe I *should* spit it out. It'd still be bigger than yours, apparently."

"Okay," Brint said as he stepped between them. "Good to see you two hit it off so well. We'll be coming back to Riq tomorrow for some language-device training." He mumbled, "That ought to be fun."

Next they were introduced to Arin, a young woman with thick blond hair. Of all the Hystorians they'd met so far, she seemed the most stressed, clutching a disorderly stack of papers to her chest.

"Arin is in charge of creating a Hystorian's Guide for each Break," Brint explained. "She's been combing through our archives, gathering the information that will be most useful to you in different time periods."

Arin shook hands with Dak, then Sera. "*Archives* sounds impressive, but what Brint means is that I've spent months rummaging through boxes full of mildewed papyrus and crumpled bamboo scrolls. There was one twentieth-century Hystorian who left behind a numbered collection of soup-can wrappers. I still can't figure out if it's an important cipher or if the poor man was simply a very organized hoarder."

Mari gave Arin a warm smile. "It's been daunting, but Arin's done a marvelous job."

"I thought I'd have more time, that's all," Arin said softly, and then she wished them luck and scurried away.

Dak realized too late that he should have thanked her. By the time he thought of it, they'd already made their way around the room, returning to the platform with the podium.

Brint turned to Dak with a satisfied smile on his face. "Now that we've done that, we want to take you to meet the people going with you on your trip. They're highly trained—"

The sound of an explosion cut off his words. The entire operations center rocked, throwing half of the people to the ground. Dak stumbled into Sera and they crashed into the wall. She wrapped her arms around him to keep both of them from toppling over.

There was a second boom, followed by another jolt to the room. This time Dak and Sera *did* fall—he landed on top of her and heard her grunt despite the ringing in his ears.

Brint and Mari both stumbled over to Dak and Sera and helped get them to their feet. For the moment the explosions had stopped, but the Hystorians were shouting, running around with panicked expressions on their faces. It was mass confusion.

"What's going on?" Dak asked. His heart rate had skyrocketed, and he noticed Sera was holding his hand. He pulled away, embarrassed.

Before anyone could answer his question, the huge monitor that dominated the room went black. When it came back online a moment later, a face filled the screen. It was a woman with flaming red hair and lipstick the color of black oil, her face all hard edges. The room hushed as everyone stared at the screen in horror.

After all was completely silent, the fierce-looking woman spoke.

"You really thought you could hide such a thing from the SQ?" she asked, her voice biting with hate. "We're coming, Brint. We're coming for your precious Infinity Ring."

15

A Hastening of Plans

THE LADY IN RED'S announcement was immediately followed by a series of shattering explosions that rattled the operations room and sent ceiling tiles raining from above. Clouds of dust arose where pieces of ceiling hit the floor. Dak cradled the Ring to his chest protectively. That nasty woman had threatened to come take it from him, and no way would he ever let that happen.

"Come on," Brint said tightly, throwing a worried glance at Mari. "We don't have any time to mess around."

He grabbed Dak by the arm and escorted him roughly up the aisle that rounded the room. Mari and Sera were right behind them—Dak noticed that Mari had retrieved the SQuare, and was hurriedly placing it back into her satchel. Brint came to a panel in the wall and pushed. The whole thing pivoted open. The four of them slipped through into a hidden room that was only about eight feet across and completely empty. Dak turned to see Riq follow them inside, then Brint shut the panel.

"Language is going to be your biggest barrier," Mari said. "We need to get that taken care of before we can send you off. We just have to hope our defenses hold until we can get you to the insertion team."

Dak tried not to show how terrified he was. "What's going on anyway? Who was that woman?"

"We call her the Lady in Red," Brint answered. "Her name is Tilda. You'll never meet a viler, more hateful woman. I don't think she cares one whit about anything except amassing power and moving up the ranks. She won't be happy until she's the leader of the SQ. And she's convinced that wiping out the Hystorians is the best way to make that happen."

"Riq, quickly," Mari ordered. "Tell them about the devices."

The teenager seemed to have lost some of his arrogance from before. *Nothing like an invasion from an evil red-haired lady to shake you up a bit,* Dak mused.

Riq pulled out several small objects from a plastic cylinder he'd had in his shirt pocket. He held up a couple of them—one looked like a headphone bud, and the other a tooth.

"What the heck are those?" Dak asked.

"While your parents spent their whole lives playing around with time travel," the young man answered, "mine worked on language-translation equipment. And this is so beyond what the rest of the world knows, you won't even believe it works."

He stepped forward and leaned toward Dak, holding out the earpiece. Dak instinctively took a step backward.

"Hey, quit being a baby," Riq said. "Come here!"

Dak had to push down his rising anger. "Fine."

He let Riq reach up and put the tiny device in his ear, shoving it down until it almost hurt. Then he put a second one in Dak's other ear.

"All right, this is the part you won't like," Riq said.

Another explosion rocked the building, sending all of them teetering for a few seconds as the room shook. When the place stilled again, Dak glared at Riq warily.

"Don't worry," the teenager said. "It'll only hurt for a few seconds."

Dak was determined not to show any more fear. "Okay, what do I do?"

"Open your mouth. Open wide."

Dak shot a questioning glance at Sera, who looked on impatiently, then did as he was told. Riq leaned forward and stuck his fingers in Dak's mouth. Dak gagged — it was maybe the least pleasant part of a very unpleasant day. There was an uncomfortable *click* that he couldn't tell if he'd heard or felt. Then a burst of pain shot through his body, and he jumped back from Riq — who was actually smiling.

But the pain went away quickly, just as had been promised.

"So what is —"

Riq cut him off. "No time to explain. You'll find out soon enough, when you're able to talk to people in different languages. It'll take some time to get used to, but you'll be fine after some practice."

Riq did the same thing to Sera, who stood still and didn't complain a lick. When Riq was finished, he stepped back and nodded to Mari.

A thunderous boom sounded, and this time Dak and the others fell to the floor. They scrambled to their feet as muffled shouts rang out from the other side of the secret panel.

"The SQ is in the HOC!" Mari yelled.

"We can't waste another second!" Brint shouted at Dak and Sera. "Get the Ring ready! You have to go now—hurry, before they storm in here and take it!"

Mari seized Brint by the arm. "Brint, we have to wait for the insertion team. They're just kids!"

"There's no time. For all we know, our team is dead."

Dak swallowed, the reality of it all hitting him hard and heavy now. "Where do we go?"

"It doesn't matter," Brint answered. "Just away from here. I'll come with you."

Mari clearly didn't like it. "Riq can go, too. You'll need all the help you can get."

"Now hold on—" Riq said.

"But—" Dak began.

"No more buts! We *do not* have a choice!"

The woman pulled the satchel off of her shoulder and handed it to Sera. "Guard that with your life. You can't do anything if you lose the SQuare! If for some reason you do, you'll have to travel back here and get a new one. But that might get messy—there's no telling what you'd be coming back to."

Dak nodded, then moved to stand close to Sera. Riq joined them, looking utterly put out. There were sounds of gunfire now in the other room. Gunfire, and screams.

"You know how to do it, right?" Dak asked Sera, his voice tinged with hysteria.

She simply nodded. He felt a pang of loss again when he handed over the Infinity Ring, as if he were throwing away his parents in some way.

Sera immediately set to work on the programming function of the Ring. Her face was a mask of concentration.

More shots rang out on the other side of the wall. A woman screamed, a sound of pain and terror. Dak felt utterly useless, knowing that if he tried to help Sera he'd only get in the way, slow her down. So he braced himself and waited for the next terrible thing to happen.

It only took about ten seconds.

The secret panel tore from its hinges and flew through the air, windmilling until it smacked into Brint. He cried out and crumpled to the ground as Mari dove for cover. Dak looked back at the now-open passage to the HOC. Two men in soldier's gear stood there with guns raised, a red beam blazing out from each of their scopes.

"Get on the ground!" one of them yelled. "Now!"

Dak dropped, bringing his arms up to cover his head—like that'd do any good if one of these thugs decided to shoot a bullet in his direction. Sera cowered in the corner, working on the Infinity Ring nestled in her lap, hidden from plain view. Riq crouched right next to her.

"How *dare* you come onto our property like this!" Mari shouted. "We'll report this to every media—"

She wasn't able to finish before one of the men struck

her with the butt of his weapon. She cried out and fell next to Brint, who lay still where he'd dropped.

A rage roared inside Dak — a fury that he never knew was possible all those years he'd spent reading in his room. That already seemed a lifetime ago. He charged the soldier who'd hurt Mari. Screaming at the top of his lungs, he dove and tackled the man, knocking him off balance. The second man was on Dak in an instant, dragging him by the hair across the floor while he kicked out with his feet and wailed from the pain.

The man dumped him into a heap. "One more move or remark that I don't like, and someone gets shot. Do you understand me? Now where's the Ring?" Dak saw in horror that the soldier had finally noticed that Sera was not just sitting there, but busy working on something. "Hey! What're you doing?"

Sera looked back at him, her face lit with fear. "Nothing. I'm just scared."

"You think I'm stupid? Hand it over!" the man yelled. "I won't ask again."

Sera had turned her attention back to the device. "Okay, just one second."

"Now, you little brat!"

He moved toward Sera, and Dak scrambled to get in front of him. He landed in Sera's lap just as Riq reached over and placed his hand on her shoulder. There was a *click* and a *beep*. The world collapsed into light and sound and they were sucked away from Hystorian headquarters.

16

Far, Far Away

SERA RELISHED the escape. The ordeal through the wormhole lasted just a few seconds, the same mind-jolt of movement and streaking turns of light and darkness, the same feeling that her atoms were about to shake loose. And then it was over without transition, that instant shift to stillness and normalcy as if nothing had happened at all. She looked around her.

She was at the foot of a giant pyramid, its huge blocks of yellow stone angling away toward the sky so that she couldn't even see its apex far above. The ground was dry and dusty, the air around them sweltering hot. She sat in the same position as she had in the hidden room outside the operations center, and the Infinity Ring rested in her sweaty hands. Dak was still sprawled across her lap but quickly scooted away to lie on the ground to her right, his head resting against a block at the bottom of the pyramid.

And Riq was standing just over her shoulder, peering up at the huge structure with such a blank expression that he could have been a wax statue.

"It's . . ." she started to say. "Do you think they're okay?"

His dazed eyes finally met hers. "Brint and Mari can take care of themselves. And I'd rather not let them down, so we've got a lot to do. No time to mess around."

Dak had sat up straight with his back against the stone. "Great. They sent the most annoying person in that whole operations room with us. Just great."

"Dak," Riq retorted, "be glad you're a little kid or I'd break your nose about five times to make myself feel better. You think I *want* to be here?"

Dak glared but kept quiet.

"Sorry," the older boy muttered. He walked away, went over to sit on a rock that jutted from the sand. "I just wasn't ready for this. There are people back there . . . I may never see again."

Sera sighed. The shock of everything had almost over- whelmed the fact that they were sitting at the foot of an actual Egyptian pyramid. And the blocks of stone looked much newer than she would've imagined, which meant they'd come far into the past, just as she'd hoped. She wanted to be as distant from the SQ as possible, both in time and geography. She looked at the imposing structure, knowing she should be more impressed, but her eagerness to get on with things outweighed all else.

She stood up and slapped the dust from her pants. She grabbed the Infinity Ring in one hand and took the satchel from Dak, then held both items out in front of her.

"Hey, look at me," she said. "We need to start using

these things the way they were meant to be used. If we do what the Hystorians asked, then maybe when we go back the SQ will never have attacked, and we'll all be living fat and happy."

"Wait a second," Dak replied, seeming deep in thought. "If we change history, then maybe we change our future lives, and if there's no need for Breaks to be corrected, then maybe we never build a time-travel device and the Breaks that didn't need fixing never get fixed and . . ." He stopped, his expression having changed to complete confusion.

Sera knew what he was getting at. "Better not to even go there. Time paradoxes are way too complicated, and we don't know for sure how they work. That's why we can't risk going back to our own time."

"We can't go home again, huh?" Riq asked.

"Not until we've done everything Brint's asked of us. What if we go back home and the Infinity Ring blinks out of existence before we've fixed all the Breaks?"

"You could make another one," Dak said. "Couldn't you?"

"You're assuming I wouldn't blink out of existence, too."

"That could happen?" Riq asked. He looked deeply troubled by the idea.

"The whole point is that I don't know! Look." She put the Ring in the satchel and handed it to Dak, then took a stick from the ground, using it to draw a line in the sand. "Time is like a river, right? That's what *time stream* means. The current is flowing in one direction—toward the future—and we're all being pulled along for the ride. The Ring, of course, lets us move upstream or downstream at will."

"Oh, goody," said Riq. "A metaphor. They didn't tell me you were a poet, too."

"Here's a poem," said Dak. "Roses are red, violets are blue. Please just shut up, why don't you?"

"I've got the speaking stick." Sera raised the stick. "And it doubles as a hitting stick, so *both* of you be quiet."

"Time. River. Got it," said Dak.

"Now imagine the Breaks as great big boulders that have been plopped into the time stream. The stream keeps flowing, but it has to veer a little bit from its natural course, working its way around the boulders. It's not a completely different river—it still gets where it was going, for the most part—but there are subtle changes all along its length. Ripples. Remnants."

"And as we remove the boulders," Riq added, "the river goes back to normal."

"Right, but we can't say for sure what 'normal' looks like. As long as we're moving from place to place with the Infinity Ring, we're anomalies, and we're immune to the changes we're causing. But when we return to our proper time . . . who knows."

"So, we won't be affected?" Dak asked. "Our memories will stay intact? And the Ring, too?"

"That's the theory, Dak. I'm sorry, but this is all uncharted territory here. All I know for sure is that the second we start changing things, the time line will be in flux and we won't be able to take anything for granted.

All we can do is make the changes the Hystorians tell us to and hope for the best. Otherwise we might go back to discover the planet is a chunk of dead rock floating through space."

Riq moved closer and eyed the satchel in Dak's hands. "Okay, fine. So how in the world do we know what to do? They didn't tell me anything about the Breaks, their locations, nothing. I started my training in The Art of Memory, but hadn't gotten too far."

"Then it's a good thing two out of three of us are smart," Dak said, stepping up beside Riq. "We'll figure it out. You just be a good boy and translate."

Riq laughed, which made Dak's face grow red. "How many languages do you know, by the way? I forgot."

"One," Dak said in a deadpan voice.

"Ah, okay. When I need help with English, I'll come to you."

"And when I need help on how to look stupider, I'll come to you."

Riq pointed a finger at Dak's ear. "Just remember, as impressive as that device is, it won't help you with reading and writing. You're basically illiterate now. Just sayin'."

Sera cleared her throat. Dak was usually so quick to trust strangers. She wondered if Riq reminded Dak a little too much of himself. "You guys finished?" she asked. They each gave the other a dirty look, but then nodded at her. "For the love of mincemeat. Dak, you can't be dumb and learn tons of languages. And, Riq, you better be nice to my best friend—he knows more about history than your bosses. I guarantee it." She waited a moment to make sure she'd put their argument to rest, then took a deep breath. "Dak, there's something else. I've been thinking about your parents, and I think they're anomalies, too."

Dak got serious, fast. "What does that mean?"

"They warped out with us, but they didn't warp back in. That means they were lost in transit. Without the Ring to steer them, they'll be completely unanchored, hopping through the time stream like skipping stones. But I don't think their movements will be entirely random. As untethered anomalies, they should theoretically be drawn to other anomalies in the time stream."

"Theoretically?" Dak echoed. "I'm getting so tired of that word!"

"What I mean to say is that I think they'll be drawn to the Breaks. Which means, as big a place as time is, there's a very real chance we'll encounter them in the course of our mission."

Dak took a moment to consider what she'd said. Then he held out the satchel. "Let's get on with it, then."

Sera couldn't have agreed more. She sat down, pulled the SQuare out of the satchel, and turned it on. Dak and Riq crowded around her to see what appeared on the screen. There were just two sentences, white letters on a black background, with an input box below them:

```
You have one chance to type password.
Fail, and device will explode.
```

17

Finger Tapping

"You're kidding me," Sera said. "All of that talking, and they forgot to give us the *password*?"

Dak had felt a little quiver in his gut, too. Here they were in ancient Egypt—he took yet another look at the Great Pyramid of Giza, still in disbelief that he was standing at the foot of something he'd dreamed about seeing for years—with nothing to guide them on what to do next except a SQuare device that was locked to them. But, man, the air smelled clean and fresh, like it hadn't been tainted by a few thousand years of humans doing what they do. Everything *looked* sharper, too. He couldn't help feeling optimistic.

"We'll just have to take a guess," Dak said. "Maybe it's *Hystorian*."

Riq scoffed. "Yeah, why don't you go ahead and type that in. Give it a whirl. If it blows up, oh well!"

Dak would've loved to punch the guy right in the stomach—if only there wouldn't be consequences, like, for example, getting beaten up in retaliation. "I didn't mean to just go ahead and do it, moron. I was throwing out ideas — maybe you should try to actually contribute something."

"I'm about to smack the both of you," Sera said evenly, and her hardened face showed she meant it. "You two haven't even known each other long enough to be enemies. Cut it out."

"Seems plenty long enough to me," Dak grumbled.

"I mean it," Sera snapped. She returned her attention to the screen. "The more I think about it, the harder it is to believe they would've sent us away with this if we couldn't find a way to figure out the password. We just need to think about it for a while. Once we agree on something, all we can do is try it."

"But it has to be logical," Riq said. "We can't take any wild guesses." He didn't look at Dak when he said it, but Dak knew it was a jab at him.

Sera turned the device off and folded her hands on top of it. "All right then. Let's all *think*. No talking for a few minutes."

Dak pressed his back against the bottom of the pyramid — *Seriously*, he thought, *how cool is* this? — and put his head in his hands, closing his eyes. He'd memorized the two sentences and ran through them in his mind. Thinking back to their short time at the Hystorian headquarters, he tried to remember if either Brint or Mari might've said something that could've been a clue to the password. But nothing came to mind.

Frustrated, he wondered if maybe the message on the SQuare itself was a clue. He pictured the words in his mind. *You have one chance to type password. Fail, and device will explode.*

"I think I might know what we need to do," Riq said. "It has to be related to explosives somehow. Bombs. Fail-safes. Bombs have fail-safes, right? A way to make sure they don't explode?"

"Um" was all Sera got out. "I doubt any of us are experts on that."

"Well," Riq replied, "maybe we can hike our way to a local village and ask someone around here about it. Get them to help us figure it out."

Dak was astounded. *"You're* a Hystorian? You really think people in ancient Egypt had bombs? Especially electronic bombs with fail-safes built into the device?"

Riq looked up at the pyramid. "Well . . . no, I suppose not. Got any better ideas?"

Dak went back to brooding with the others. He closed his eyes again to block everything out. Then it hit him, fast and hard. "I've got it!" he yelled, standing up.

Sera and Riq jumped at his sudden exclamation, and Dak relished the briefest hint of wounded pride that flashed across his new rival's face.

"What?" Sera asked. "Spit it out!"

"We're thinking too much," Dak said. "Just like anyone else would. But because we know absolutely nothing about this, there's no *way* they'd let us risk destroying the thing by guessing at passwords. So they told us what to do, right in front of our eyes!"

He saw a flicker of understanding in the others, and he hurried to spit out the solution before either of them could claim they'd figured it out, too. "Password. We need to type that word. *Password*. That's it."

Sera and Riq exchanged doubtful looks.

"What else could it possibly be?" Dak asked them.

"That's really risky," Sera finally said. "What if it's wrong?"

"Duh!" Dak threw up his hands in frustration. "What if any word we come up with is wrong? Got any better ideas? It seems obvious to me."

"I think he's right," Riq said—which irritated Dak slightly, because it made it harder to hate the guy. "If we only have one chance, it would have to be something that stands out once you see it. And that does. Plain and simple."

Sera slowly nodded while biting her lower lip. "I guess I'm just scared to death to actually try anything. We only have one shot."

Dak shrugged. "That's why *you* should type it in. Go for it."

"Why not you?"

"Because I'm the history expert. They need me. Badly."

"I think you mean history *nerd*," Riq muttered under his breath.

"Well, technically you're right," Dak said. "As any real language expert should know, the origin of the word dates back to the mid twentieth cent—"

"Maybe later," Sera interrupted. "As engaging as that sounds, let's focus on this right now."

"Okay," Dak said. "Hand it over, I'll do it." He had a burst of confidence that he was right about what to input. Taking the device from Sera, he took a seat and turned it on. The same two sentences popped up on the screen. He drew in a breath, tapped the box, typed out "Password" on the virtual keyboard, then clicked the OK button.

The screen instantly flashed white, and for about half a second Dak thought it was the beginning of a massive explosion that would incinerate him. But then words started to appear.

```
Break #1


Sally forth, astute and wise
Search the page, find the prize
Centuries pass, mind and heart
Devoted to the Memory's Art
```

Dak smiled. "What did I tell you? I solved it with my eyes closed."

But his victory was short-lived. Below the poem was the most confusing image Dak had ever seen, a hodgepodge of circles and broken lines and shapes. There were Greek letters on one side of the image, and the word "lagoon" on the other.

"What the heck is *that*?" he asked.

"Spain," Riq whispered. "We need to go to Spain."

18

Bye-bye, Pyramid

"HUH?" SERA asked. "What hat did you pull *that* out of?"

Dak had just been about to ask the same thing. Nothing in the weird picture seemed to suggest Spain. Or anything else for that matter.

Riq was obviously trying to hide a satisfied smile — but not too hard. It sneaked its way across his face. "They gave us something easy to start with. I could've done this one after just a couple of lessons."

"Lessons in what?" Dak asked.

"I told you before — The Art of Memory."

Sera was nodding. "They mentioned that to us, but didn't say much about it."

"It's an image-based memory trick." Riq pointed to the screen. "It's been scrambled up beyond recognition, but if you imagine rotating the pieces around, you can see it's the Spanish coat of arms."

Dak leaned in for a closer look. If he squinted, he could almost make it out. "Spain, huh?"

"Not just Spain," Riq said. "But a city and date, too.

The Greek letters actually stand in for numbers — a common practice. And *lagoon* in Latin is *palus*. We need to go to Palos de la Frontera on August 3, 1492."

Dak recognized the time and place. There was only one possible explanation for why they'd need to go there.

"Hey, you in there?"

Dak blinked — Sera was snapping her fingers under his nose. "Sorry, just accessing the genius shelf in my brain. I know what we need to do."

Sera's eyebrows rose, and even Riq looked intrigued.

"There's an obvious candidate for a Break, something that ends up affecting the entire world for centuries, all the way up to now. Or then. Or when it used to be our now. You get me?"

"Yeah, we get you." She rolled her eyes a bit. "So what is it?"

"That's where the ships leave that'll eventually discover the Americas. The *Niña*, the *Pinta*, and the *Santa María*. The voyage of the Amancio brothers!"

"Good. Let's get there, then we can see what else the SQuare has for us," Sera said.

"Works for me," Riq said.

Dak felt like leaping in the air and kicking his feet together — he was so excited. But he figured he better act like the mature save-the-world man he'd become, so he simply nodded and said, "Let's get her done."

Sera shoved the SQuare into the satchel then pulled out the Infinity Ring. As she fiddled with the programming, Dak moved his gaze to the Great Pyramid towering above them, slanting up and away as if it went all the way to the sky. He thought of the thousands of people who'd worked on it, performing superhuman feats with massive stones that would've been difficult to move into place even with modern technology.

"You know," he said, that comforting and familiar urge to share his great knowledge warming him from top to bottom. "Funny story about the Egyptians. When the royals died, it was very important to prepare the bodies so that they could last forever, mummify them until they were ready to rise up as gods in these humongous tombs. One thing they did was take their *brains* out, *through* their nose. Now that's one big booger. The way they did it was—"

"Dak!" Sera yelled. She smiled when he looked back down at her. "That's so . . . *vastly* entertaining, but . . ." She held up the Infinity Ring.

"Time to go?"

"Time to go."

They gathered around her and touched the Ring. She pushed the button and the Pyramid was yanked away in an explosion of light.

19

Clothes and a Poem

SERA WAS on her back. She opened her eyes to see a perfect blue sky, only a few wisps of clouds flecked across its surface. A warm breeze blew up and over her body, along with the sounds of crashing waves. She sat up to see a stunningly beautiful ocean, the water blue and dark and choppy with whitecaps, several old-timey sailing vessels out on the horizon.

"Wow," she said, gripping the cool metal of the Infinity Ring in her lap. "That's awesome. The waves are a lot bigger here than at the beach where we go with your mom and dad."

"That's because we go to a bay," Dak answered from her left. He sounded bitter, and she wondered if mentioning his parents had been a bad idea.

"Yeah, I know. Sorry." She slipped the Ring back into the satchel.

Riq was sitting cross-legged to her right. "Did everything come through okay? The SQuare? The Ring?"

Sera pulled out the SQuare and inspected it. "They look fine."

He gave a satisfied nod then turned to look behind them. Sera did so as well. Several small wooden buildings sat a few hundred feet away, and behind them an entire village. People milled about, but it didn't seem like anyone had noticed the visitors from the future yet.

Sera got on her feet and brushed the sand from her pants. Looking at them made her think of how much they would stand out. "First thing we need to do is find some new clothes."

Dak was already pointing at a small house on the beach. "Look, they've got a bunch of laundry hung out to dry. Perfect!"

"That's called *stealing*," Sera chided.

"Are you kidding me? Small price to pay for saving the world from destruction and mayhem. They'll have great grandkids who'll thank us. Come on."

"Now wait just one second," Riq scoffed. "I'm not going to run around following two little squirts excited to dress up and play history together. This is serious business, and we need to think things through."

Sera didn't want a long argument. She knew Dak had a point about the clothes, but figured saying so wasn't the way to get Riq on board. "You're probably right," she said. "Maybe we shouldn't worry about the clothes. Let's just hang out for a while. Talk it over and hope no one spots us."

Riq looked at her suspiciously. "Well . . . when you put it that way . . . I think we should probably grab those clothes after all. But just don't do anything stupid!"

He took off in that direction, slipping and sliding in the sand, and Dak was right on his heels. Letting out a sigh, Sera went after them.

A half hour later, Sera, Dak, and Riq were crouched behind an old barrel in an alley on the outskirts of the village. They'd stealthily made their way up from the house on the beach. Some of their newfound clothes—thieves, all three of them!—were too small, some too big. But they'd found just enough to get by. The boys wore linen shirts covered by buttoned jackets that Dak called doublets, with breeches and hose that looked ridiculous to Sera. But not as bad as the twill housedress she had to wear—completely impractical and bulky.

Dak wore a hat as well—low crowned with a wide bill—and kept straightening it, breaking into a smile every time. She knew that he was living a fantasy he would've never thought possible just a few days ago. Literally living history. She wished she could be just as excited—but all that occupied her mind was stress and worry.

"Time to check the SQuare for a hint, don't you think?" Dak said after they'd spent a minute or two spying on the people walking through the streets ahead of them. "If we don't find a Hystorian for help, we're sunk."

"That's punny," Riq whispered.

"Huh?" Dak responded.

"Never mind."

Sera turned and sat down on the ground, then pulled out the SQuare. She flicked it on and the strange diagram—the Art of Memory puzzle—had been replaced by a short menu:

```
Access Granted
The First Break - Menu
   Daily Journal of Activity
   Hystorian's Guide
   Identify Break
   Locate a Hystorian
   Proceed to Second Break
```

"Seems simple enough," Sera said. "Dak, you're the history nerd in this group, so you'll be in charge of keeping the journal. Just think, if we make all of this happen, you'll be one of the most famous Hystorians ever."

Instead of coming back with a smart aleck remark, he smiled pridefully. "That sounds like a job I can handle. But it makes me a little sad to think we're changing the thing I love so much."

"We'll just be making it better. Right?"

Dak nodded, though he didn't appear so sure.

Sera tapped the screen and frowned. "Wait. Something's wrong."

"What is it?" Riq asked. Dak seemed to be daydreaming about his potential role in history.

"I clicked on the 'Identify Break' option, and look what happened."

```
Data Corrupted
Return to previous menu?
```

"That's not good," said Riq.

"When the SQ attacked," Sera said, "everything went crazy, and Mari had to yank this thing right off of the main computer. What if she was uploading data? And what if the upload was incomplete?"

"Then we might be in trouble," said Riq.

"Relax," said Dak. "We know it's got to have something to do with the Amancios. We can work it out."

"Try something else," suggested Riq.

Sera went back to the menu and tapped on "Locate a Hystorian" as Dak and Riq leaned in to see over her shoulder. A short message appeared, and Sera let out a sigh of relief.

```
If you've solved the puzzle to arrive here,
in both time and place, the following riddle
will help you find the person you need. If
you've made a mistake and have gone some-
where else, then you are royally bunked.
Good luck.
```

Sera had just finished reading it when the words faded away and were replaced with a poem:

```
A wee little bee flies through the sky
It stings your nose and makes you cry
```

And run on a road till it comes to a tee
Looks out at the bright and brilliant sea
It's her, you scream, the way it ends
That's how you must find your friend

"Hmm," Sera said. The other two made similar sounds as they all stared at the six lines of the poem. Dak even went so far as to scratch his chin, purse his lips, and widen his eyes — he looked like a mad scientist.

"Any ideas?" Riq asked.

"I've got a few," Dak replied, still not losing the comical expression. "Studying the Renaissance era was a hobby of mine for a few months back when I was six. I'm sure that'll come into play here."

Sera had to repress a groan — of course, she had no room to talk. She'd first discovered her love of quantum physics when she was four.

She'd also been raised speaking Spanish at home, but she was worried about Dak's ability to interact with the local Hystorian when the time came. "What do we do about these translation devices in our mouths and ears?"

Riq gave a slight shrug. "Well, it would've been nice to train you on them for a while, but they're not that hard. They're linked together by radio frequency, and the earpiece can judge almost instantly what language it's hearing. It'll translate for you automatically, and trigger the tooth device to alter your words as they come out of your mouth — which means that in each new setting, you want to let someone else speak before you do. The speaking part's a little tricky; it takes some practice to know how slowly to speak and when to pause, that sort of thing. But the translation of what others are saying—that works like a charm. Maybe let me do the talking as much as possible until you get the hang—"

"Well hello!" someone barked from behind them, cutting Riq off.

Sera turned her head to see an enormous man with a dark beard. He held a long iron bar in one fist, bouncing it in the palm of his other hand. Sera's heart froze.

The giant took a few steps forward, then leaned down to sneer at them.

"I never thought I'd see it," he said with creepy awe. "Visitors from the future."

One-sided Conversation

DAK JUMPED to his feet, dragging Sera to hers as well. Riq stood right beside them as the man took another step closer. He could now reach them if he decided to swing that big iron rod in his hands. And probably not for just a love tap, either.

"Who are you?" Riq asked.

"Who am *I*?" the man responded gruffly. His lips didn't move in sync with the words Dak was hearing, which meant the translator device was actually working. Even in the face of certain death by a barbarian, that was pretty cool. "Three little urchins show up in the streets of my town, dressed in ill-fitting clothes, looking as out of place as an anvil in a cooper's shop, and you ask who *I* am?"

There was a long moment of silence before Sera said, timidly, "Yes?"

The man let one end of his rod fall to the ground and he leaned on it like a cane. Then he laughed, a deep bellow of a noise that almost made Dak look up to see if it was going to rain.

"We can explain everything," Sera said. "It's not what you think."

"Not what I think!" the man roared. "I just said you were from the future and you didn't bat an eye or protest! That something you think people go around talking about?"

Dak reached out and pulled on Sera's hair. Talking to this guy was craziness — they needed to run. She looked at him sharply then returned her glare to the stranger.

"I'll tell you who I am," he said. "I was trained by my father, who was trained by his mother, who was trained by her father, who was trained by his mother. From there it goes three mothers in a row and then a string of fathers. Way, way back is my point."

"Trained to do what?" Dak asked.

"To look for the likes of you, that's what. I'm a Time Warden of the SQ, raised to the Watch when I was only fourteen. But if I'd known the people we've been looking for all these centuries were nothing but a few weaned babies, I'd have left the honor to my little sis. Who has one arm. And no legs."

That pricked Dak's pride. "Well, if it's any consolation, we were hoping you'd be shorter," he grumbled.

"Why are you here?" the Warden asked. "What do you know?"

Sera opened her mouth then closed it. She seemed to be considering reasoning with the giant.

"Look," she said at last, "we know who you work for. They don't care about anybody but themselves. We *are* from the future and, trust me, they make a mess of everything."

"Who cares about the future?" the man rumbled. "They're paying me well *now*."

"We can pay you!" Dak exclaimed. "Do you accept, um, currency from a country that hasn't been established yet?"

"What I want from you is your reason for coming here. What are you planning?"

If only they *had* a plan. But that reminded Dak: They did have the riddle. He was confident he could work it out, and that would mean they'd have an ally in the village. But he needed to buy some time. And some distance would be nice, too.

"Speak!" the man shouted. "Speak or I'll start breaking faces with my toy!"

"Okay, okay," Dak said. He felt a funny flutter in his mouth when he spoke and something like a double-echo in his ears. His translation tool would need some practice if the goal was to fit in — assuming they survived the next five minutes. "We can tell you everything you need to know."

"You sound funny, boy."

"Dak, what're you doing?" Sera whispered fiercely to him.

He just winked at her in response. Then he stepped forward so that he was directly beneath the angry glare of their visitor. He held his hands up. "I'm using a translation device, so if I sound funny, it's his fault." He jabbed a thumb back at Riq. "You're right — we did come from the future, and we came in a very complicated travel machine. It's hidden under the sand out on the beach.

We'll take you there if you promise not to hurt us."

"And we have laser guns," Riq blurted out. "Touch us and we'll zap you. Zap you to death!"

Dak spun to give him a hard glare. "Um . . . yeah, those. Very dangerous." He turned back to the Time Warden. "So the time machine's that way."

The man's face hadn't so much as twitched during the exchange. "Time machine? Laser guns? What is this nonsense?"

"We're from the future," Dak responded. "What do you think we did, snapped our fingers and *poof*? Time is a river; we came in a boat. It's that way."

When the man finally let down his guard and turned to look in the direction Dak had indicated, Dak went for it. He lurched forward and slammed his shoulder into the Time Warden's side, knocking him off balance as the iron bar rattled to the ground. Then Dak pushed him again, and the man toppled over.

As the Warden roared in rage and scrambled to get up, Dak grabbed Sera and Riq by the hands and yanked them in the opposite direction. Without looking back, the three of them sprinted away and around the nearest corner, into the busy streets of Palos de la Frontera.

21

A Pile of Boxes

SERA COULD hear the shouts of the Time Warden behind them like the rumble of thunder as they ran, causing all the people bustling about to stop and stare at the commotion. Sera and the others pushed and dodged and zigzagged their way through the crowd. There were men and women, many of them carrying baskets or sacks. Carts and animals, children chasing one another, sellers hawking their wares. She kept one eye on Dak, hoping he had some kind of plan—besides "run!"—in that precious brain of his.

They passed a shop with cuts of meats displayed in the windows and approached a tavern, where a large group of people had just exited, filling the street. They'd just started shoving their way into the mass of people when Riq was suddenly lifted off his feet and backward. He shrieked in surprise, and Sera spun to see what had happened. The huge bearded man had caught up to them, had grabbed Riq by the back collar. He slammed the teenager to the ground and lifted a fist to punch him.

Sera snapped. She screamed and jumped on the man, wrapping one arm around his neck. He threw her off and into a pack of people. They broke her fall, put her back on her feet. She looked just in time to see Riq, still on his back, kick out with a foot, slamming the man in the shin. A roar escaped his lips.

A second later, Dak charged in, ramming once again into the Warden's side with the knob of his shoulder. The man tumbled to the ground as Dak helped Riq back to his feet.

"Make way!" Sera yelled, pushing a path through the crowd. The three of them sliced their way through, leaving their stunned enemy to regain his wits. They broke free from the throng and picked up speed once they were in the open. Angry shouts from the Time Warden rose up behind them as Dak took the lead again.

After a minute of hard running, he rounded a large cart and horse then ducked to the right, in between two high walls that separated a tannery and a cooper's shop. Riq and Sera followed — Sera was terrified they were letting themselves get trapped, but there wasn't any time — or breath — to argue. They reached the end of the long, narrow alley and entered a backstreet, bordered by a filthy stream. Dak found a stack of abandoned wooden boxes, then slipped behind them. Sera squeezed in next to him, and Riq did the same.

No one said a word — all of them trying desperately to quiet their heavy breathing. The Time Warden couldn't have been too far behind, so if he'd noticed where they'd gone, he'd be on them within a minute.

Two passed. Three. Four or five. As the time stretched on, a calmness settled over Sera. Maybe they were safe. Maybe they'd lost him.

"We did it," she whispered.

Dak gave her a worried smile. "Yeah, but now we know he'll be looking for us. It really stinks that we can't walk around the village and enjoy the sights a little."

She blinked at him. "Are you serious? That's your biggest concern right now?"

"Hey, we might see my parents, too! You said they'd be drawn to the Breaks. What if they're here?"

Riq cut in. "Our biggest worry is solving that riddle and finding a Hystorian. If we can't do that, what does it matter?"

"Well," Dak said. "Who's got an idea?"

"I think we should go to the local beekeeper," Riq offered. "Seems pretty obvious to me."

"The beekeeper?" Dak scoffed. Then he was off. "Okay, okay. Sometimes it pains me to have to explain such obvious stuff to people, but at least you were smart enough to know that beekeeping was a big deal in those—in these—days. Without the development of sugarcane, they needed the honey—plus the beeswax was vital for the candle-making industry."

"Right," Riq said, his voice full of annoyance. "I figured as much. So why are you talking to me like I'm an idiot?"

Dak looked flabbergasted. "Because. Hello? Towns and cities didn't have beekeepers! That was all done in the abbeys and monasteries, nowhere near a place like this. Good grief."

"Well, aren't I just the dumbest person who ever lived?" Riq asked.

"Do you really want me to answer?" Dak said.

"You guys, seriously," said Sera. "For the love of mince—"

Just then something clicked. Like a lock falling into place inside Sera's mind. The words of the poem clarified in her thoughts. "Don't worry," she said, trying to hide the rush of excitement. "I got it. I know the answer."

"What?" Dak asked. "You do? How? Who is it? Where?"

Sera grinned. "Our Hystorian is a butcher."

The poem had no real meaning—it had just been trying to spell out a word. "Bee" in the first line. "You" in the second. Then "tee" and "sea." BUTC. And finally it said that it ended with "her." BUTCHER.

It took a while to explain, but in the end Sera just hushed their questions. If she was wrong, they'd keep looking. For now their problem was making it to the butcher without being spotted by the Time Warden.

"I'll take the lead this time," she said. She realized she was clutching the satchel at her side in a tight fist, as if someone might snatch it away if she didn't. "You two keep a lookout while I decide which way we should go."

"Okay," Dak whispered back. "But if you get us killed, I'm gonna kill you."

"Deal."

She poked her head out and peered around. Down the little lane there were a few kids throwing garbage into the stream, but no one else was in sight. She remembered that the butcher's shop was right next to the tavern and inn they'd seen, and if her sense of direction was right, they could make it most of the way there without returning to the main thoroughfare. She slipped out of their hiding spot and started running, crouching down as she did so. She could hear the soft footsteps of her friends behind her.

She came to another alley that led back to the main street. Coming to a stop with her shoulder pressed against the rough wood, she slowly leaned forward and took a peek. Other than people going this way and that on the far side, she saw nothing but a couple of stray chickens pecking at old bread.

"All clear," she whispered before taking off again.

They repeated that process three more times before coming to the end of the lane. They had no choice now but to walk through the alley to their right and enter the main thoroughfare of the village again. Sera's heart picked up just at the thought of it. The Time Warden was probably roaming the street, bouncing his menacing iron rod on his open palm.

She took a step into the alley when Dak grabbed her by the arm.

"What do we do if he sees us?" he asked. "We can't run to the butcher and give the Hystorian away."

"In that case, we'll have to split up," Riq suggested. "He can't follow all of us."

Sera shook her head. "I'd rather blow the Hystorian's cover than get separated. We don't split up for anything, and we don't leave anyone behind. Now let's go."

She jogged lightly down the alleyway and slowed when she approached the end, glancing quickly over her shoulder to make sure Dak and Riq followed close behind. The noises of the main road rose to a pitch—laughter and horse's hooves clopping on the cobblestone and sellers yelling for potential customers. She was just about to peek around the corner when the huge body of the Time Warden suddenly filled her vision—his chest at her eyes and his face towering above.

"Well," he bellowed. "I knew the rats would come out soon—"

There was a loud thumping sound as his head jerked forward—his eyes rolled upward, and then he collapsed into a heap on the ground. A woman with long brown hair stood directly behind him, a large wooden club gripped in both of her hands. She wore a white apron with bloodstains all over it. Her chest lurched with heavy breaths.

"I knew something was up when I saw this lug chasing people," she said.

"*You're* the butcher?" Dak asked, the surprise evident in his voice.

The woman held the club out in front of her as if inspecting it. "Never leave home without one of these—it can knock out people just as well as cows." She returned her gaze to Sera and the others. "Yes, I'm the butcher. But more importantly for the likes of you, I'm the local Hystorian. My name is Gloria."

22

A Sharp Pair of Scissors

DAK WANTED to ask a million questions as the woman—who wielded her club like a knight wields his sword—led them to her shop. But she shushed him, told him to wait. People along the street gave them odd looks as they walked by, but none that lingered enough for him to worry too much. They reached the place they'd seen earlier, by the inn, and went through the front part—filled with hanging carcasses and wooden tables and lots and lots of knives—into a back room that held a few chairs.

Gloria motioned for them to have a seat, and then she took one herself after hanging her bloody apron on a hook. Dak couldn't help but notice how everything seemed more intense in the past—by the ocean, everything had seemed sharper and fresher, but in this cramped room, dirt was dirtier, smells were smellier.

"So," she said. "There's no need to beat around the bush too much. I've been trained for this day, but I have to admit I never thought it would come. I'm just going to ask you a simple question, and I want a simple answer. You ready for it?"

Dak nodded, as did the others.

Gloria leaned forward and put her elbows on her knees. "Are you from the future?"

"Yes," Dak said immediately. "We're from the future." He had to keep himself from smiling at the very idea.

"Good," the woman responded. "You look out of sorts, quite honestly, and the man who was chasing you comes from a long line of SQ thugs. I won't bother with the usual 'I can't believe it' and the 'you can't be serious' mess. I swore my life to this cause, and I'll accept it now that I'm seeing it." A broad smile spread across her face.

"Pretty cool, huh?" Dak said, letting his own smile come through now. He could see the kidlike excitement in the woman's eyes, and he knew she was a true ally.

"What's it like?" Gloria asked. "The future where you come from?"

Sera and Riq seemed more than happy to let Dak answer. "In some ways it's amazing. We have airplanes—they're like ships that fly—and ways to talk to people on the other side of the planet as if they were sitting right next to you. There are huge buildings that are hundreds of spans high. We've even sent people to walk on the moon."

Gloria laughed, obviously thinking that last one a joke. Dak decided not to press it—he thought back to the warning from his parents. Not to step on any bugs in the past.

"But things are getting bad," he continued. "Lots of earthquakes and hurricanes and other scary stuff. Plus, the SQ is stronger than ever, pretty much ruling the whole world and running it into the ground. Aristotle was right—we need to fix the Breaks."

Gloria's look of wonder dropped into a gloomy stare. "Which is why you're here. And I'm in this city for a reason, so I can guess why you've come."

Dak was curious. "What would your guess be?"

"A little young to be interrogating your elders, no?" She smiled. "I'm sorry, this is just such a . . . *momentous* occasion, I don't feel quite like myself."

Dak shrugged. "It's okay. I've never really had a chit-chat with someone from 1492, so it's all good with me."

"There's a major voyage planned for this week," she said. "Commissioned by Queen Isabella herself, and led by Christopher Columbus. Does it have something to do with that?"

"Yes!" Dak shouted as he stood up. He quickly recovered and sheepishly sat back down. "Oh, sorry. I get a little excited about this stuff. But yeah, that's my guess, too. There should be three ships—the *Santa María*, the *Niña*, and the *Pinta*. Their voyage ends up being really important. If history is about to go off course, our best bet is that it'll have something to do with those ships."

"Hold on," said Riq. "Who's Christopher Columbus? Aren't we talking about the voyage led by the Amancio brothers?"

"Well, sure. The Amancio brothers—Salvador and Raul—were in charge once they threw Columbus overboard," Dak answered. "The mutiny can't be the Break, can it? No way. I've always read that Columbus was the bad guy."

"Maybe the mutiny is *supposed* to happen and we have to help it," said Sera. "If the SQ prevents the Amancio brothers from discovering America, that could cause all kinds of trouble with the time stream. Gloria, have you ever heard of them?"

"I know of Salvador and Raul. They're relatively popular in the court of Ferdinand and Isabella. Respected. But what on earth is America?" Gloria asked. She'd followed their exchange, her eyes widening with each word.

Dak was only too happy to give her a history lesson. Except, oddly enough, he was telling her about the future. "It's hard to believe I'm in a time when people don't know about this. Those ships are going to do a whole lot more than find new trade routes for Spain. They're going to stumble upon a major continent that will come to be known as the Americas. It's a whole New World, Gloria. It's where we come from."

Gloria considered for a minute. "You think you need to make sure the mutiny happens as it's supposed to. It's that simple?"

"Well . . ." Dak said. His enthusiasm dimmed—there was really nothing *simple* about the situation. "I'm not sure how this whole Break business works yet. But we definitely need to get on that boat. It can't be a coincidence that we were sent to this time and place. That voyage is the key."

Gloria turned an eye on Sera and said the strangest thing. "Then we'll need to give you a haircut."

It turned out there was a reason Gloria had been the Hystorian assigned to the port town of Palos de la Frontera when their suspicions about the SQ's presence there had arisen. She was extremely knowledgeable of the shipping industry and had major contacts with all the fleets. She knew the only way to get Dak, Sera, and Riq on board the ship would be to pass them off as scrub hands. And that meant sticking to a no-girls-allowed policy, which Sera did *not* take very well.

"How can they be so sexist?" she asked as Gloria brought out a very nasty looking pair of silver scissors. "And have you even *given* anyone a haircut before?"

"Sexist?" Gloria repeated. "I don't know what that word means. And the only hair I ever cut is on an animal, right before slicing it wide open. I promise I won't do that last part to you."

"Gee, thanks."

Gloria started snipping away.

Dak watched all of this with a constant urge to snicker. Riq sat by a window, lost in thoughts he didn't care to share with anyone, hopefully looking out for any sign of the Time Warden's burly frame. Gloria had called in a favor to have him thrown into jail, where his story of time-traveling rascals wouldn't win him any friends. But it wouldn't be long before his bosses heard about what had happened and had him sprung. Time was of the essence.

Dak was still confused by the Break business. "We're here to *change* history, right? Maybe we could try to talk to the Amancios somehow before the voyage."

"Not much chance of that," Gloria answered as she cut free a big handful of Sera's hair. "First of all, how would you get to them? Second, even if you did, why would they trust some goofy-looking kid? Mutiny is a very serious offense, and the last thing you want to do is scare them into changing their minds unless you're positive of what needs to happen. You might be doing the SQ's dirty work for them."

Dak churned with indecision.

"Ow!" Sera suddenly shrieked.

"Oops," Gloria responded. "Sorry—sometimes I forget how long these blades are."

"So how are you going to get us on the ship?" Dak asked.

The Hystorian eyed him for a second, then went back to her cutting. "I know the man in charge of hiring urchins and thieves to do the dirty work—they always need people at the last minute. And a catch of three strong and able boys will make his day, I promise."

"I'm hardly a *boy*," said Riq.

"You're more of a boy than I am," said Sera.

"Strong and able?" asked Dak.

For the first time since they'd met her, Gloria looked worried.

23

Behind the Bandana

THE SUN was sweltering when Gloria took Sera and the others out a back door and saddled a couple of horses she had tied up in a small stable. She'd prepared satchels with bread and grapes and dressed them in clothes she said belonged to her nephew. She also smudged dirt from a little garden all over their faces and clothes—Dak smiled the whole time, crowing about living history; Riq grumbled and complained about "going native." Gloria *tsk*ed at his complaints. She insisted that they needed to look a lot less like nobles, and fast. It was customary that hired hands spent the night before launch on the ship itself, so they had no time to lose.

Sera was a nervous wreck, and it didn't help that she hated what Gloria had done to her—dirt was one thing, but she felt completely naked without that comforting sense of hair on her neck. She still had enough to wear a ponytail, but just barely. Fortunately, men of the period didn't wear their hair *too* short.

"Hey, you make a pretty convincing boy," Riq said

to her after she was all dirtied up. He smiled to soften the blow.

"You don't," she replied, but gave a smile back.

Dak finally joined Gloria on one horse — after three failed attempts to get up in the saddle and a whole lot of complaining that the bicycle hadn't been invented yet — and Sera sat with Riq on the other. He tried to sit in front but she refused — it was already humiliating enough for her to pretend to be a boy. She'd at least have the satisfaction of taking lead on the stupid animal. Why was she in such a bad mood? Just because of a haircut? She tried to convince herself it wasn't because Dak was raring to go for a sailing adventure with the famous Amancio brothers and didn't seem scared one bit.

Once they were all mounted up, Gloria turned her horse to face Sera's. "I know an out-of-the-way path that'll get us to the port house where we should find my friend, Stonebull. I'm not expecting any trouble, but if we cross paths with that Time Warden or any of his friends, there'd be no point in fighting. These horses are swift, and we'll have to rely on their legs to save us. If we can reach Stonebull, we'll tell him that the Warden is just someone you stole food from and who wants revenge. He won't care a bit about that — he'll simply be happy to have a few extra hands to replace those who inevitably chicken out on the last day."

"We'll be lucky if *Dak* doesn't chicken out," Riq murmured from behind Sera.

Dak heard it. "We'll be lucky if they don't have the ugly

police inspecting anyone who tries to come on the ship."

"Why?" Riq responded. "Then you'd have an excuse not to go."

Dak didn't miss a beat. "Yeah, I know—they only allow ugly people on these voyages. Duh."

"Are you two finished?" Gloria asked. The woman seemed completely bewildered by their behavior.

Neither of them acknowledged her, but they also shut up.

Sera liked that the two of them had resumed picking at each other. For some reason it gave her a sense of comfort and familiarity. And she was starting to think Riq wasn't so bad after all. Anyone who could keep up with Dak just might be a friend for life.

"Glad that's settled. It's this way." Gloria started off down a path leading to the woods behind her butcher shop.

Sera gave her horse a light kick and followed.

As they rode through the trees, Sera kept hearing tidbits of conversation from Dak and Gloria about history—Gloria's future. For the most part it amused Sera, but she was a bit appalled when Gloria turned to her and asked, "Is he telling the truth? The world travels around the *sun*?"

How could anyone actually think the Earth was stationary? They obviously knew nothing about gravity and centrifugal force.

They eventually left the woods and went up a long, sandy hill, then crested a rise and stopped when a stunningly beautiful bay came into sight below them. Sera almost gasped at how breathtaking a view it was — greenish-blue water, bright buildings lining the hillsides surrounding it, majestic ships with sails furled, floating in the harbor. No one said anything, but a quick look around showed Sera that the boys were just as impressed.

"We'll be at Stonebull's in a matter of minutes," Gloria announced as she got her horse walking again.

They'd gone out of their way to avoid the eyes of the Time Warden — who may very well have been freed by then — or anyone who might work for him, swinging away from the main road and coming back again where it met the sea. As they entered the cobbled streets, there was still no sign of trouble. But Sera was wary — if Gloria could guess why they might have come to this time and place, so could the SQ.

"Here it is," the Hystorian announced. They had stopped in front of a plain-looking wooden building with steps and a small porch. Gloria swung off her horse. "Come inside with me so you won't be sitting targets." She tied the reins to a hitching post after Dak jumped down. "Like I said, it shouldn't be too hard to get you three on that ship."

Sera followed Gloria's lead up the steps and through a rickety door. There were a few tables and chairs inside, but no people. The place smelled like sweat and beer.

"Just a minute!" a man yelled from a back room—the door stood slightly ajar. "Just takin' care of me bidness, if you know what I mean!"

His accent was strange, almost a mixture of several that Sera had heard before. It made her wonder if Riq's device was having a hard time deciding how to best translate his words.

A gruff-looking man walked out, hitching up his dirty trousers. His shirt was filthy, too. And his face and his hair and his hands. Everything about him. He also hadn't shaved in a few days. But none of this was what stood out most about him.

He only had one eye. And it was a big one, as if it wanted to make up for the lack of its partner—where the other should have been, there was nothing but a big, mangled scar. He had a bandana tied around his head and, noticing everyone gawking, he quickly pulled it down to cover the injured spot.

"Sorry," he grumbled. "Forgets that it ain't the prettiest sight sometimes. Pardon me mishap, if you will. Now, what can we do for you on this fine-weathered day?"

"Where is Stonebull?" Gloria asked.

"Down at the bay, I 'spect. Keeping an eye on the ship's loadin'. Asked me to fill in for him for a spell. So here I am, lookin' at you fine folk, askin' what you might be needin'."

If Gloria was put out by the change in plan, she recovered quickly, motioning at Sera and her friends. "I rounded these troublemakers up for you—they're desperate for money, and I know you're probably looking for some last-minute additions to the help."

"Right we are," he said quietly as he looked the three potential workers up and down. "Right we are. Can't say as we're all that picky, neither. You three willin' to work yourselves to the bone? Sleep little, sit little, eat little, sick up that what you do? Get yelled at and kicked in the tush now and then?"

Sera wanted to say something contrary, but she couldn't risk her voice giving her away. She nodded, and saw the others do it, too.

"Well, that's good enough for the likes of me," the man said with a chuckle that revealed several missing teeth. "And blessed be your little bottoms—I'll be joinin' you on this fair journey to the far reaches of the hungry sea. Hope you're up for it."

Gloria narrowed her eyes. "You're going on the voyage, too? What are you doing on the ship?" she asked.

"Why, I'm the taskmaster, that's me. In charge of all the lowly workin' folk. The name's not important." He took a step forward and pulled up his bandana to reveal the hideous scar again. "They just call me Eyeball."

2 4

Up the Gangplank

DAK COULDN'T imagine a more perfect companion on his first voyage across the ocean than Eyeball. Quirky, crude, a vicious scar on his face — probably from a battle with pirates — what more could he ask for? And the taskmaster might be just the right man to seek help from as well. He'd be respected. He'd know everyone on board, and the ins and outs of how things worked.

And if the very sight of the man made Riq visibly uncomfortable, well, that was just a bonus.

"No time to waste," the man said, grinning his gap-toothed smile again. "My things are already up on the beast, and by the looks of it, you three ain't got much more to your names than a bag of clothes and all your eyeballs. Be thankful for that, by the way. Having just one ain't as easy as it might look. *Look.* Get it? Ha! Let's go."

He'd been stepping toward the door as he spoke, a slight limp in his right leg. Gloria quickly gathered Dak and the others in a huddle.

"I know this has all happened quickly," she said, "but we didn't have much choice, did we? The Hystorians are asking a lot of you, but I have faith. I've barely met you, but I already believe you can do it. Get on there, learn things, scout it out. Find out what the SQ is up to, and do whatever it takes to stop them. Understand?"

Dak suddenly remembered one of the last things his dad had said to him: This wasn't a game. Not only were they walking right into a violent mutiny—and planning to somehow involve themselves—these voyages were scary enough to begin with. The whole crew never survived a trans-ocean trip in these days—a few dozen would probably die from disease alone. Happy thoughts to begin their journey.

And he couldn't help but feel conflicted about changing the past. Changing the thing he loved most. Could they really take the Hystorians' word on *everything*?

He realized everyone was looking at him. "I'm totally excited about this. Let's do it."

"Okay, then," Gloria said with a motherly smile. She pulled each of them into a hug and then stepped back. "I wish I could be of more help. I wish I could go with you, but you know I can't. Good luck, and remember: The fate of the world lies in your hands."

Dak laughed. "No pressure or anything, right?"

"Hey!" Eyeball barked from the open door. "If I stand here much longer, I'll have to take care of me bidness again. Let's get!"

A flurry of panic swirled through Dak, but he pushed

it down. This was it. His chance to literally live history. The right path would present itself.

"Thanks, Gloria," he said. "One day there'll be a book about how you helped us save the world."

And with that, he walked out the door, trusting the others to follow, and hoping he was right.

Eyeball led them through the streets, dodging carts and people and kids who darted around like fish. Their guide didn't say a word, just kept moving with that limp and a grunt every now and then when he saw something that he seemed to take unkindly to. But he never bothered explaining. Dak stayed right on his heels, enjoying every second.

They turned a corner at a large wooden inn, and Dak almost stumbled when he saw the ships docked in the bay suddenly rise up before him. Each mighty mast seemed to touch the blue sky far above, with pointed beakheads at the front and squared off sterns in the back. They looked just as he'd seen them in countless illustrations. People swarmed all over the ships like hungry ants searching for a spare crumb, and shouts and whistles filled the air. Somewhere, men were singing.

"There she is," Eyeball said, his voice full of pride. He was pointing at the largest of the ships. "*La Santa María de la Inmaculada Concepción*. Destined to do great things, that beauty. If she weren't made of splintered wood and filled with sweat and grease, I'd marry her and have lots of babies."

"For the love of mincemeat," Sera muttered. "Not a good image."

The man didn't seem to hear her. He kept walking, head held high as they got closer and closer. A gangplank had been laid out, and two roughnecks with knives in their belts stood guard at the bottom of it. They didn't flinch or make a move for their weapons when Dak's group approached, which could only mean they knew Eyeball well.

"Afternoon, you buckets of lard," the taskmaster said to them. "Got a few of those extra recruits Stonebull's been hoping for. These ugly little runts ought to do."

"Hey!" Sera said in protest. But then she quickly shut her mouth, and Dak hoped her higher voice hadn't made the men suspicious.

"Shut up, you little weasel!" Eyeball roared. Then to the guards, "That one hasn't hit the age yet, but he'll work hard enough. I'll make sure of that."

"You slugs better be up to workin' right away," one of the guards said, a tall man with a ridiculous mustache. "Lots to do before setting sail tomorrow. Slack on the job and you won't be aboard when we go."

"We'll make you proud, sir," Dak said enthusiastically before he could stop himself. Riq groaned next to him and Sera gave him a dirty look. Dak hardly noticed.

"Up with ya, then," the other guard said, before launching a long, slimy spit into the ocean water.

"Follow me," Eyeball said. He stepped between the two armed men and started walking up the long plank.

Dak motioned for Sera to go next, then Riq. Dak wanted to savor every moment of this. He'd forget for now that they could very well be dead in a few days. With a deep breath of satisfaction, he headed up the narrow strip of thick wood.

The ship seemed so much bigger now, almost like a living thing — especially with the workers moving about every last inch of it. There was even a guy working on the furled sail at the very top of the mid mast, looking as if he'd fall to his death with the slightest wind or misstep.

Dak stepped onto the lower deck of the ship, where his two friends were straining their necks to take it all in. Eyeball was talking to a group of men in hushed whispers, one of whom stood out from the crowd. He was tall with broad shoulders, and dressed much nicer than anyone else. He had that look about him that said he expected people to do whatever he told them to do.

The man suddenly stepped away from the group and approached Dak, looking square into his eyes. Dak realized he'd been staring. Squirming under the man's gaze, part of him wanted to turn and run back down the gangplank. But he stood his ground and waited to see what would happen.

"Welcome aboard the *Santa María*," the man said, holding out a hand. Dak timidly took it, and the guy about ripped his arm off shaking it. "My name is Christopher Columbus."

Scrub Scrub

HISTORY HADN'T been kind to Columbus. Those few stories that even acknowledged his existence didn't paint him as the nicest guy. But now, with so much at stake, all Sera wanted in all the world was to not get kicked right off of the man's boat.

She had seen this look in Dak's eyes before, after all. They were wide and dazzled . . . which meant he was about to do something really stupid.

"I can't believe I'm actually meeting you," her friend said. "The books I've read have been critical, but—"

Sera kicked him in the shin to shut him up.

"Ow!" he shouted, jumping up and down while he held his leg. "What was that for?"

Columbus let out a huge laugh. "Oh, how I love the stupidity of these kids you bring on the ship, Eyeball. They remind me of my own son." Then he switched from amusement to fierceness faster than Sera could blink. "Now get them working! And I better not see any more of this horseplay, or we'll have people in the brig by the time we launch tonight!"

With that he stormed off, shouting orders left and right as he went. Sera saw him kick someone in the rear end.

Dak looked at Sera, almost sad. "Guess you *have* to be a jerk to lead a ship full of thugs."

"You want to give us away?" she whispered back to him. "Careful what you say!"

"Hey, that rhymed."

Sera wanted to strangle him.

"You poppycocks done?" Eyeball asked roughly. "Embarrassed me right in front of the captain. I ought to dash your brains out and throw 'em overboard."

"We're really sorry," Sera said. "My friend is just excited that we're here and got a little carried away. We're ready to work."

A huge grin spread across the man's face. Several of his teeth looked rotten and about to join their long-lost partners. "That's good, then. 'Cause you're gonna be worked to the livin' bone."

Eyeball lived up to his word.

Sera spent the next few hours working harder than she'd ever done before. And it mostly involved crawling around on her hands and knees, scrubbing the wood of the upper decks. Every last muscle in her body ached. Dak was helping her, and Riq was behind them spreading out pitch—a black tarlike substance that sealed the wood and protected it from water.

Despite having the easiest job, Riq complained the

most. But they didn't talk much, because every time they did, someone would yell at them to shut their traps and get back to work. It had become impossible to tell who was in charge anymore, but everyone on board seemed to have the right to boss them around. Eyeball showed up every now and then, threw out a few swearwords for good measure, and then he'd disappear again.

Sera was scrubbing away when she heard voices above her. She looked up to see a couple of men fixing a rip in one of the sails with some thick twine and a large needle. She couldn't quite tell what they were saying, but she thought she heard the name "Amancio," and one of them was pointing toward the back of the ship.

She nudged Dak, then turned to look. Two men — one short, one tall — were making their way along the decks. They both had long black hair and shirts that revealed their entire arms, which were ripped with muscle.

"Those're the Amancio brothers," she whispered.

"You're right," he said back. "I've seen paintings, and that's definitely them! The tall one is Salvador, the shorter one Raul."

Sera flicked a glance at Riq, but he was too far away to join the conversation. "What do you think? Is this mutiny supposed to happen or what?"

"I don't know. We need to snoop around and learn more, I guess. We've only got a few days before they do it."

"Huh? How do you know that?"

He gave her his special look that said, *How can you possibly doubt my infinite wisdom?*

"Slacking on the job, are we?" a voice said from behind them.

Sera spun to see that the Amancios had stopped directly in front of them. The taller one — Salvador — leaned over and put his hands on his knees.

"So you're the ones old Eyeball brought in for us today, eh?" he asked. The man smiled, and he looked way too kind for someone about to throw the captain overboard. "Well, work hard and you'll do great things here."

He straightened, and then his brother Raul spoke. "Great things indeed. You're going to be a part of history, boys. Is this your first voyage?"

Sera and Dak, both a little starstruck, only nodded.

Raul looked out at the distant sea, where the sun was almost ready to dip below the horizon. "Ah, there's nothing more invigorating than the open sea. You pips are gonna love it."

The two of them marched off, stopping to talk to each worker they passed.

Sera looked at Dak and raised her eyebrows. "Did we just get a pep talk?"

"I kinda like them," he said, then got back to work.

Sera did the same, her shoulders aching with every push and pull of the brush.

They worked into the evening, right through the launch of the ship, which Dak was devastated to miss. But Eyeball had a talent for showing up every time Dak attempted to sneak off to the ship's railing. He was still

139

grumbling about it an hour later as they scrubbed by the light of lanterns. They'd finished most of the area they'd been assigned when Eyeball appeared again, seemingly out of nowhere.

"I heard you met the Amancios," he said. "They approve of you wretches, I reckon."

"They said that?" Sera asked, feeling a little burst of pride.

"Ha! No such thing. But they didn't throw your tails off the ship, so that says it rightly enough. Now come on. You've barely done a blastin' thing, but it's time for a meetin' with the captain."

Barely done a blastin' thing, Sera repeated in her head. She fought an urge to poke the man in his remaining eye. But it was all she could do to walk straight on the bucking, rolling ship.

The meeting he'd mentioned was for the whole ship. Nearly three dozen people packed onto the lower deck, body to body from fore to aft, some having to climb up onto the masts and rafters to fit. Christopher Columbus stood on the highest deck, looking mostly down on his men. *And, unknowingly, one girl,* Sera thought. The Amancio brothers stood to each side of their boss, which made Sera feel a prickle across her shoulders. The captain had no idea what history had in store for him.

Then Columbus began the meeting with a statement that emptied her head of all other thoughts.

"Listen up, crew." His voice boomed through the night. "It's come to my attention that there's a mutiny planned on our voyage."

2 6

Listening Ears

THE REST of the meeting was a bunch of noise to Dak. He couldn't focus, could barely hear over the chatter going on all around them. Columbus said something about how there'd be no stopping him, that the voyage would go on as planned. Dak wanted to look at Sera, talk to her, but he knew it'd be risky. Every eye on the ship was now searching faces for clues that might reveal who the scheming culprits could be.

And Columbus seemed even more like a pompous jerk than he had before.

Dak's heart raced and his mind spun. Was their mission already jeopardized? What *was* their mission?

Columbus had grown quiet and was waiting for the crew to do the same. Shushes hissed through the air until everyone finally went silent.

Their captain leaned forward, his face grave in the lantern glow. "There'll be no mercy. No quarter. Anyone who plots against me will be thrown overboard. Anyone who *reveals* those who plot against me will have their pay doubled. I've put Salvador and Raul in charge of this matter, so all suspicions and reports should go directly to them. For now, we will get our rest. You are dismissed."

The crowd erupted again into sound, everyone talking over everyone else, bustling about and heading this way and that. But Dak couldn't move. The Amancio brothers were in charge of investigating their own planned mutiny. He didn't know if that helped or hurt his task. Sera stepped in front of him, a forced smile on her face.

"Well, shall we find our spots to sleep?" She said it loudly, with a piercing look in her eyes that said he needed to snap out of his stupor. Now was not the time to look out of place. Someone would suspect them.

He shook his head to get the cobwebs out and then nodded. "Yeah. Yeah, we better."

Eyeball appeared then, having pushed his way through the crowd, barking orders as he went. When he saw Dak and Sera, his eyebrow arched above his lonely namesake. "You two lookin' a mite tired, I'd say. Better rest up before the sun pops her head over the horizon and says boo. Gonna work you to the bone again. You'll see."

"Where do we sleep?" Sera asked. "Nobody's shown us our room."

Eyeball exploded in a fit of booming laughter. "Your room? Your *room*?" He paused for another round of guffaws. "You'll be sleeping on the splintery floor with a dozen other louses like yourself. Now get belowdecks before I change me mind and make it the floor of the sea."

Dak and Sera rushed off, rejoining Riq and following a small crowd of others who looked as pathetic as they. Down the ladders they went, into the stinky bowels of the ship.

As they descended, Dak noticed that Salvador and Raul had come along, not far behind, then broken off to go somewhere else. Before Dak could think about the danger, he grabbed Sera and Riq by the hands and led them in the direction the brothers had gone.

"What's our plan?" asked Riq in a low voice.

"I don't know," whispered Dak. "But they're probably going to talk about what just happened, right? Maybe we can listen in. Maybe we can offer to help with their investigation, so we can figure out who's on which side."

They rounded a tight corner just as a cabin door thumped shut ahead of them. Neither of his friends protested as he crept up to the door—in fact, they followed him, crouching close to listen. Dak's heart pounded like a gorilla trapped in a cage—they couldn't risk this for long. The three of them leaned in and put their ears against the wood.

The voices were too muffled to reveal which brother was which, but their words were clear enough.   .

"It's going to be tougher than we thought."

"How did he find out? I thought we'd rooted out all the spies."

"I don't know. But this better be the last time we have to do all the dirty work."

"You know it will be. We'll rise quickly up the ranks of the SQ once this is done."

Dak's heart had slowed, but it was also breaking. He'd known deep down that this was probably the reason they were here — that the mutiny was one of the Great Breaks, that it never should have happened — but it still hurt to hear it.

Heavy footsteps sounded, and the three of them straightened up and scurried away from the door — a good thing because Eyeball came thumping around the corner.

"Burn me crusty lid!" he roared. "Where'd you lumps go off to?"

Riq spoke quickly. "Sorry, sir. Somehow we took a wrong turn. Can you help us?"

Eyeball scrunched up his face, but he looked more annoyed than suspicious. "Dumber than a cured slab of ham, you three. It's back this way." He jabbed a thumb over his shoulder.

They headed that direction, Dak's head buzzing. There was no doubt what they had to do now. Dak. Sera. Riq. The Three Pathetic Musketeers.

They had a mutiny to stop.

27

Riffraff

THEY ENDED up in a corner of a low-roofed room that would've looked cramped and uncomfortable *before* a dozen people packed inside of it. Two low-lit lanterns hung from the rafters. Each member of the crew had been given a scratchy wool blanket, and Dak and Sera now sat with their backs against the rough wood of the wall, people of all ages around them. Riq was just a few feet away, already lying down, his chest slowly rising and falling.

"How'd he fall asleep so fast?" Sera asked. It was the first they'd spoken since Eyeball had chased them off. But the shock of the dreadful news they'd learned — and what it meant for their mission — was evident in her eyes.

Dak shook his head back and forth mockingly. "The little cowboy is all tuckered out. Hey, I guess there's not a shower on board, huh."

Sera wrinkled her nose. "Imagine how bad this place is gonna stink in a week."

"A week?" Dak asked. "Try a couple of months. These voyages aren't like Caribbean cruises, ya know."

"What's your story?" someone said.

Dak looked over to see a boy, just a couple of years older than him by the looks of it. He was filthy, and the ship hadn't even left yet.

"Our story?" Dak repeated. He didn't feel ready to use his translation device to make friends quite yet. But it was now or never—they'd need help if they were going to mutiny against a mutiny. "Just needed some work, like everybody else."

"How about you?" Sera asked. "What's *your* story?"

"Got nothin' else in life. My name's Ricardo." He nudged the boy to his right, a darty-eyed kid with messy hair. "This is Francisco. And this is Daniel." He gave a jerk of the head to his left. Daniel was much older, but had a blank look on his face that made him look young.

"Where are you from?" Dak asked, but immediately regretted it. He didn't want the same question returned to him.

"A small village about a hundred miles from here. Decided maybe we should skip town when the mayor put a price on our heads."

The boy named Francisco spoke up, wiping the hair out of his eyes. "Like all our thieving was such a bad thing. People's gotta eat, right?"

"People's gotta eat," Daniel followed up, a goofy grin on his face. "Or people's gotta die."

"Where are *you* from?" Ricardo asked. "Your accent is . . . weird."

Sera opened her mouth to speak but Dak hurried to

cut her off, scared she'd get something wrong. "We're immigrants. Been all over. Never settled." He flashed a quick look at Sera, trying to communicate that being vague was best.

"Got stories to tell, I bet," Ricardo said. "Stories to hide. Doesn't matter. We're all the same now. Brothers, startin' all over."

Dak nodded. He liked this guy. "That's right. Brothers." He elbowed Sera just to rile her a little. "This one has been a brother to me since before I can remember."

Sera elbowed him back, much harder. "Yes. I can't tell you how many times I've had to save *this one* from getting his throat slit or his face beaten in by thugs. Not the strongest boy, I can tell you that. Ugly as a burnt stick, too. But he's all I got."

Ricardo and his two friends looked from Sera to Dak and back again, their expressions somewhere between surprise and delight. Then they all burst into laughter.

"It's gonna be a long voyage," Ricardo said when the chuckles died down. "It'll be good to have friends. Especially if this rumor about a mutiny is true."

Dak's smiled vanished at that. Reality struck home. "Hey, what do you think about all the people lumped with us? Any chance . . . you know, that they could be involved with the plot?"

Ricardo scoffed and smacked his friend Francisco in the head, ruffling the boy's mop of hair. "People like us? *This* riffraff? No way. We're the dried scum on the bottom of the bucket."

Dak took a second and scanned the room, searching their company, barely revealed by the soft light of the lanterns. Shaggy hair, ratty clothes, dirty faces, rotten teeth. The lowest of the low, with no aspirations but to earn a next meal. This was exactly what they needed.

He brought his attention back to Sera and their new friends. "How much can we trust you?" he asked Ricardo.

The boy held out his hand. Dak shook it.

Ricardo gave a stiff nod. "Completely. If you're alone on a voyage, you might as well be dead. Why are you asking? Why so serious all of a sudden?"

Dak looked at Sera, who he knew understood the thoughts going on in his head. Both of them had doubts about their mission, even after hearing firsthand that the Amancio brothers worked for the SQ. It didn't help that Salvador and Raul seemed all right, while Columbus seemed like a jerk. But the fact of the matter was this: The SQ ruled the world of the future with an iron fist, and the Cataclysm that Brint and Mari had spoken of seemed to be coming faster and harder with each passing day. Dak and Sera had experienced the evidence up close and personal.

They were Hystorians, and it was time for action.

Dak, his resolve solid, faced Ricardo again. "Riffraff is a good name for this group. We might need to turn them into an army."

Awake in the Night

SERA HAD always known that she and Dak shared a special link. As different as they were, they thought alike, and often came to the same conclusions. And she'd shared his line of thinking over the last few minutes.

They were here to do a job. Going to Columbus with what they'd learned was out of the question — there wasn't much of a chance he'd take their word over the Amancios'. Which meant they'd have to get directly involved. But if they were going to stop a mutiny, they'd need help. And the sorry bunch of runaways and criminals surrounding them might be their best shot at finding any. Especially since the SQ probably paid them no attention. Looked at them as powerless and therefore worthless.

"What's this army stuff about?" Ricardo asked Dak. "Why ya need such a thing?"

Sera leaned forward and whispered in Dak's ear. "Are we sure about this? Totally?"

"Hey, no secrets," Ricardo snapped. "Not a good way to start."

Sera sat back. "Sorry. I was just making sure. This is a big deal."

"I think it's okay," Dak said. "We don't have much time—it's supposed to happen soon."

"What's supposed to happen?" Francisco asked.

Daniel—the older man who looked lost in a world of his own—suddenly laughed. "Sun'll go down, I bet. Then the moon'll come up." He laughed again, this time with a snort.

"Oh, jeez," Ricardo said, but his tone was more playful than annoyed or embarrassed. "Our friend is a lot smarter than he looks. Aren't you, Daniel?"

"Two plus two is four," the man responded. "Four plus four is eight. Take away the four times two and zero is your mate."

"Huh?" Dak asked.

Sera liked the man. There was a twinkle in his eye that said he knew more than he was letting on—that maybe he didn't know how to socialize and this was how he'd learned to make up for it.

"*Anyway,*" Ricardo said. "What were you getting at?"

Sera decided it was time to go for it. If they were going to do something about fixing this Break in history, they needed help and they needed to get started.

"You heard what the captain said," she began. "That there's rumor of a mutiny planned. Well, we actually already knew that and . . . we're here to stop it."

"How could you possibly know about it?" Ricardo asked. "Did someone send you?"

Sera hesitated. Telling the complete truth was *not* an option, but maybe she could avoid lying, too. "Exactly. We have friends in high places and they sent us here, secretly. I know it'd be impossible to prove everything to you, but we know exactly who is plotting against the captain."

"Who?" Francisco asked, his eyes alit with interest.

"Would you rat brains shut up!" someone yelled from across the room.

"Sorry!" Sera answered.

Everyone in the group scooted closer together and leaned in. Sera couldn't help noticing Ricardo smelled of fish as Dak started whispering even more quietly. "It's the Amancio brothers. I know, I know—hard to believe since they've obviously earned the captain's trust. But it makes sense if you think about it. Pulling off a mutiny isn't easy, so you'd need someone high up to be in charge of it. Otherwise it'd be difficult to make the rest of the crew follow the new leaders once it's done."

"Do you know what they're planning?" Ricardo asked.

"From what I've re—" Dak stopped, and Sera knew he'd been about to say something about what he'd learned in history books. Fortunately, he'd caught himself. "We were told that three days after we launch out to sea, the two brothers are going to take the captain in the middle of the night, gag him, bind him, and throw him overboard. The next morning, they're going to blame the disappearance on two *other* officers, men who are fiercely loyal to Columbus, then throw them off the ship before anyone really knows what's going on. Just like that, we have new leaders and the voyage keeps on truckin'."

Sera winced at that last word. She might not be a history buff like her best friend, but she was pretty certain they didn't have trucks in the fifteenth century.

"Wow," Ricardo said. "Serious? That's all supposed to go down three nights from now?"

"Yep."

"And how do you know all this again?"

Sera answered. "We have very good sources and powerful bosses." She hoped that it was enough.

"Who do you guys work for?" Francisco asked. "Come on, you can tell us."

Sera looked at Dak, eyebrows raised.

"Let's just say we're looking out for the interests of Queen Isabella," he said. "She believes in Columbus, and we believe in her."

Ricardo grinned. "And you believe she'll come through with a handsome reward for your loyalty, I bet."

"Then you'll help us?" Sera asked.

"Oh, we'll help you. Won't we, boys?"

Francisco nodded, shaking his mop of hair again, and Daniel laughed, which from him evidently meant yes.

"Good," Sera said. "Let's get some sleep. Tomorrow we can scout around, learn some things, maybe even get some evidence. Then tomorrow night we'll see if we can rally the rest of the people down here."

"Sounds good," Dak said, and the others all nodded.

Sera wrapped her blanket around her shoulders and lay down, squirming and twisting until she found the least uncomfortable position that she could manage. She still had the Infinity Ring tucked away in the satchel, which she kept strapped around her body and cradled to her stomach. She expected to have a hard time falling asleep, but all that scrubbing from earlier caught up to her and pulled her into dreamless oblivion.

The world was dark when she was jerked awake, a rough, callused hand gripped tightly over her mouth. Someone had her arms pinned to the hard floor below her. She struggled, tried to free herself, tried to scream, but it was all pointless. All she could hear was her own muted whine.

Then a voice whispered in her ear, the breath hot. "Shut your trap or I'll slit your friend's throat. Now."

Sera stopped, went completely still. She couldn't see a thing.

"That's a good lad. Now you're coming with me, nice and easy. If you scream when I let go, it won't be pretty."

The hand left her mouth, then she was pulled up and onto her feet. Someone stood behind her, keeping her hands clasped painfully in the small of her back. She heard the smack of stone against stone, saw a spark, and then a lantern lit up, its flame small but casting enough light for her to see a man standing just a couple of feet away, regarding her coldly.

With one eye.

The Brig

"LOOKS LIKE we have some talkers in our midst," Eyeball said. "Talkin' about things that ain't none of their bidness. And . . . *spying.*"

Dak and Riq were right next to Sera, held by two more of Eyeball's thugs. She couldn't even move enough to turn and get a good look at them.

A few people had awakened on the floor around them, including Ricardo. She eyed him, trying to warn him to keep quiet. The thought crossed her mind that maybe he had betrayed her and Dak somehow, but the look on his face was genuine shock. With some fear thrown in.

"Nothin' to say for yourself, eh?" Eyeball asked with a sneer. "At least you've got some gumption, I'll give you that. Take these brats to the brig and make sure they don't get no breakfast."

Sera concentrated on not crying as the burly men dragged her away.

She didn't think it possible, but they went even deeper into the ship, to a dank, smelly pit that had several small cells along its length, each outfitted with bars and chains. All of them were empty, which didn't surprise Sera considering they had just left the dock. They had the honor of being the first criminals of the voyage.

Eyeball opened up one of the cells and the men literally tossed Dak, Sera, and Riq into it. Sera landed with a thump, smacking her head against the wall. She cried out, the first sound she'd made since being taken. Dak grunted then rolled up into a ball, moaning with pain. Riq lay on his stomach, his head nestled in his arms as if he were asleep.

There was a rattle of chains then the click of a lock. Sera looked back to see Eyeball staring down at her through the bars of their new prison.

"Tsk, tsk, tsk," he chided them. "I should've known you three wastrels were up to something when you came beggin' to get aboard at the last minute. And sneaking around like that. The only reason I don't throw you on the docks right now is because I want you in me sight. Answerin' me questions when the time's right for askin'. I hope you three enjoy discomfort and pain."

He turned and left, hanging his lantern from a hook before disappearing up the rickety ladder with his three goons.

Sera crawled over to Riq, who hadn't moved yet. Dak's moans at least told her that he was alive.

"Are you okay?" she asked, gently shaking Riq's shoulder.

He rolled over onto his back. Sera gasped when she saw the hideous swelling of his right eye, the puffy skin already turning purple.

"One of his thugs punched me on the way down here," the older boy said in a strained voice. "For no reason — I wasn't resisting."

Even though they'd all been mistreated, his almost childlike explanation just about broke her heart.

Dak groaned again, wincing from some unseen ache. "I thought I liked that stupid cyclops."

"I wonder what happened," Sera said. She showed Riq how to tilt his head to maximize the blood flow for his aches, then moved to sit against the damp wood of the wall. "I knew we should've been more careful in there. Someone obviously heard us and tattled."

Dak's face was all scrunched up in pain or anger, or both. "This would make more sense if we were plotting *against* the captain, but we were talking about *saving* him. I guess the Amancio brothers have allies everywhere."

"We should've been more careful," Sera repeated in a deadened whisper.

"I'll say," Riq replied. "I rest my eyes for one minute and you two go and botch the whole mission." He gingerly prodded his swollen temple. "I guess there's nothing for it but to use the Ring to get out of here, then warp back in. Assuming you haven't mislaid it."

"No, I haven't mislaid it," Sera said bitterly. She pulled the Infinity Ring out of the satchel, happy that she'd kept it on her while sleeping — and that Eyeball clearly hadn't expected it to hold anything of value. "But we can't just hop around with it. It's out of the question."

"What are you talking about?" asked Dak. "That's our ace in the hole!"

"Do *you* want to do the calculations? Look, this thing doesn't just move us around in time. It lets us travel through space, too. Every time we use it, I have to input global coordinates—while compensating for the rotation of the Earth, the Earth's orbit around the sun. . . ."

"So you're saying you can't figure it out," said Riq.

"I'm saying that there's no way I can transport us back onto a moving ship. So unless you want to end up in the Atlantic Ocean circa August 1492, we need another plan."

"We need to break out," Dak said, as if he'd just announced he needed to use the bathroom. "That's it."

"No problem, right?" Sera said. "Just break on out. Okay, go ahead and do it."

Dak frowned at her. "Don't be a smart aleck. I'll come up with something." He leaned his head against the wall and closed his eyes.

"I'm sure you will," Riq muttered. Impossibly, he was snoring a minute later.

"What a weirdo," Dak said. "He could sleep on the tip of a weather vane."

Sera smiled sadly, and looking at her best friend, everything going down the drain, she thought of his lost parents. "I'm so sorry about your mom and dad."

Dak seemed surprised, but grateful. "Thanks. I just . . . I just hope we can figure this out and maybe help them."

"Yeah, me, too." She thought of her Remnants, and how they might stop if they pulled off a miracle and managed to fix all the Breaks. Again, she wondered if it was better not to have them, or to at least hold on to those pseudo memories. Either way, she felt like she lost.

She sighed and put the Infinity Ring away, then tried to get comfortable. Maybe her mind would work better after a long nap.

She woke up later to the sound of rattling metal.

Dak was shaking the prison door back and forth, the iron hinges squeaking and squawking against the wood. But the door only moved about a half an inch in each direction. It was obviously doing no good.

"Chill!" Riq yelled at him, scrambling to his feet. "You'll rip your own arms off before you get that door open."

Dak took a step back. "Just wanted to get my mid-morning workout in. We've gotta figure out a way to get this thing open. And is anyone else in the mood to upchuck with the boat bobbing up and down like this? Blech."

"It's probably worse being down here where we can't see outside," Sera said. She stood up to join him, examining the chain and lock, then the bars that went from floor to ceiling with a gap of only a couple of inches along the bottom and top.

"It doesn't look very promising," she said. "But the three walls are made out of wood—maybe we can do

something with that."

They each took a wall and started inspecting. Sera crawled along the back one, which she assumed was part of the ship's hull because of its slight curve and dampness. As soon as she had that realization, she stopped—it wouldn't do much good to escape into the ocean and sink the ship while they were at it.

"I might've found something," Dak announced.

Sera had just turned to see what he meant when there was a sound of hands and feet scuffling down the ladder. She looked to see Ricardo jump down the last few rungs and land solidly on his feet. He ran over to the cell, his face tight with worry.

Sera and the others rushed forward to talk to him.

"What's going on?" Dak blurted right before Sera almost asked the same question.

"They're gonna kill me if they catch me down here," Ricardo said through heavy breaths. "But I needed to tell you something. We found the kid who ratted you guys out and made him spill everything. He said that when the Amancio brothers were told about you . . ." He stopped and his face grew pale.

"What?" Sera pushed.

Ricardo swallowed. "They ordered you be killed tomorrow morning."

30

Bread and Water

"DEAD BY morning. Just in time to get rid of us before their big mutiny," Riq said.

Dak knew that he should be terrified—that he should go curl up in a corner and bawl his eyes out. But the immediate threat did something else to him—it made him realize he couldn't waste one more second feeling sorry for himself or it'd be over for everyone.

"What're we gonna do?" Sera asked. She looked at him and her eyes were hard. She knew the stakes.

Dak tried to clamp down on his panic. "Okay, Ricardo. Get out of here before they catch you. Sneak around and see if you can find us some weapons. Anything we can use to stop this from happening. Hide them where you can get to them later. Then you need to talk to every person you can trust—anyone loyal to Columbus. You'll have to use your judgment. Don't give out too many specifics, just in case. But we need to act tonight, as soon as the crew is asleep. Have people ready."

"At least now you know we were telling the truth,"

Sera said to Ricardo. "The Amancio brothers obviously want to silence us."

The boy nodded. "I'll do what I can up there. But what about you guys?"

Dak grinned—no one else knew about the discovery he'd made right before Ricardo had dropped in on them. "Don't worry. We'll be there to help."

"Now go!" Sera yelled.

Ricardo ran to the ladder and shot up the rungs.

"That's it?" Sera asked. "For the love of mincemeat, that's your grand escape plan?"

"You got something better?" Dak pulled on the board again, felt it give an inch or so. It ran along the bottom of the wall between their cell and the one next to it, and if they could pull it all the way free, he thought maybe they'd be able to get another board loose, too. Just enough to crawl into the next cell—which was unlocked.

"No, I don't," Sera responded as she gave the wood her own tug. "But this thing seems pretty solid, loose or not."

"Let me try," Riq said, already gently pushing Sera aside. "You kids don't have fully developed muscles yet."

Dak felt he had to say something back to preserve his dignity. "Well . . . you don't have a fully developed brain, so I guess we're even."

"Good one," Riq said blankly.

"Yeah, good one," Sera added.

Dak smiled as if he'd meant for his comeback to be lame. "All right, tough guy, show us how manly you are and pull that thing free."

Riq tugged and tugged, but the board didn't move any more than it had for the others. Dak almost felt elated, until he realized this was their only chance of escaping certain death.

He sighed. "We'll just have to keep working at it. Take turns so our fingers don't fall off."

"Looks like we have all day," Sera said.

Riq kept yanking on the stupid board.

Three hours later, the piece of wood had come loose another inch. It had started to make an ugly screeching sound with every pull, and Dak's head was aching from the noise. They shifted turns about every ten minutes, but it was starting to seem hopeless.

At one point while Dak was working on it he heard the sound of someone coming down the ladder and he had to jump away from the wall in a hurry. It was Eyeball, carrying a loaf of bread and a small pail of water. Two guards were with him, looking utterly bored out of their minds.

"Here you go, you louses," Eyeball said. "I was tempted to let you starve until we threw you overboard, but me softer side shone through. I'm a beacon of light, I know."

One of the guards keyed open the lock and pulled the chains loose. Eyeball stepped forward and threw the bread inside—Riq caught it. Then the man set the small bucket of water on the floor.

Dak tensed, seriously considering hurling himself at Eyeball. But the armed guards made him think twice.

"Eat," the man said. "Nothin' more tasty in this world than bread and water. Don't you fret now—we'll be enjoyin' a nice rabbit stew in the captain's hall." He smiled and winked his one eye. "Lock 'em in."

The guard repositioned the chains around the bars, pulled the links tight, then locked them in place. The three men disappeared up the ladder.

Dak was the first to the water, dying of thirst. He picked up the pail with both hands and drank steadily for ten seconds.

"Hey, save some for us!" Sera yelled. "And what about germs?"

Dak smacked his lips and let out a satisfied sigh, then handed the water to her. "Serious? Germs?"

"I was just kidding." She took her own long gulp.

"That was the most glorious thing I've ever tasted," Dak said.

Riq divvied out the bread and they wolfed that down, too. And then it was back to work on the stubborn board.

By the time evening came—which they could only guess at because they were far from any sign of the sky outside—they'd given up. Dak sat against the opposite wall and stared at the board that would bend but not break. He didn't speak, and neither did anyone else. The depressed mood was almost like a living thing—a monstrous, invisible creature that shared their cell, sucking the life out of them.

They'd have to rely on Ricardo now. Dak and the others could use the Infinity Ring to escape to another time and place, hoping that their warnings would be enough to spark a mutiny against the mutiny. Riq had figured out where they needed to go next. Sera had programmed the Ring for a quick exit. But Dak hated that idea, *hated* it. He didn't even want to know where they were going next. They'd come here to do a job—trusted by the Hystorians—and if they failed . . .

"What if we go back to before we boarded the ship? Could we stop our past selves from getting on board?" He asked it without any enthusiasm.

"It's way too dangerous," Sera replied. "Interact with our past selves? Have two Infinity Rings coexist in the same place? Time and reality are too fragile. It's probably why the Breaks have done what they've done in the first place."

"Well, thanks for the encouragement," Dak muttered.

"Uh, it's not my fault how the fabric of reality works." Sera shrugged her shoulders.

They lapsed into a lonely silence.

At some point, Dak fell asleep. He didn't know how

much time had passed when he was awakened by the

sound of chains. Groggy, he rubbed his eyes and saw that Eyeball was standing there. The man had already opened the lock and was working to remove the chains from the prison door.

Dak jumped to his feet, suddenly more awake than he'd ever been. This was it—they'd come for them. He turned to Sera, who was pressed against the far wall, eyes wide open.

"Hey," he said, "get the Ring out. We need to . . ." But then he stopped. Eyeball was *alone*. And there were three of them. They could take this guy easily.

But Eyeball's next words put a stop to Dak's scheming. "Need to travel back to the future, eh? Or maybe farther into the past?" He finally got the chains loose and opened up the door, its hinges creaking. "Poppycock. You didn't think Gloria would let you on this blasted chunk of wood without making sure you had a friend aboard, did you? Come on, now—it's time to save this ship."

31

Window to the Soul

"DON'T SIT there like a wart on a witch's nose," Eyeball said. "Come on!"

"B-but," Sera stammered. "How . . . why . . ." She didn't even know where to begin.

The man laughed. "Oh, wash my boots, kid. . . . I've been puttin' on an act 'cause you never know what side the guards are on. Gloria and I were even careful back in town—SQ's been crawling like lice all over the docks for weeks. But she sent word ahead while you lot took the scenic route. Besides, I'd have hoped you'd seen my crystal clear heart through the beauty of my glorious eye. Now come on. I've learned enough meself to know we gots to stop this mutiny."

Dak looked like his jaw muscles had been removed.

"Dak?" she asked, nudging him with an elbow.

He finally snapped out of it. "I'd just . . . I'd kind of given up. But then you came along by yourself and I was hoping we could beat the tar out of you. And now you're letting us out. I'm a confused boy." But then a huge grin lit up his face. "Let's do this thing."

"Beat the tar out of me, huh? What a dumb kid."

"Finally, someone's said something that makes sense," Riq said as he walked out the open door. Sera followed, butterflies swarming in her gut. This was it. They were finally at crunch time and she couldn't pretend it wasn't scary.

Once they were all outside of the cell, Eyeball gathered them round and spoke in a low voice. "I noticed that smelly boy, Ricardo, sneak down here this morning. So I approached him—oi, does that bloke stink like fish or what?—and told him I was on your side. He didn't believe me—I thought his rank little heart might explode on me—until I showed him some weapons I've hoarded over the last couple of voyages. By hoarded, I mean stole. Anyway, he's done a fine job of gathering your Riffraff army, as he calls it. Did I mention that boy smells?"

"Yes," Sera said. "You did. Never noticed it myself."

"Then there must be somethin' clogging that little nose of yours. Try pickin' it more often. Works for me."

"Ew" was all Sera could get out.

Eyeball got serious. "We don't have much time. Since word's gotten out about their plan, the brothers are planning to strike at midnight—I've got me own spies about, you know."

"How do we know you're on our side?" Riq asked.

Eyeball looked hurt. "Why in the blazes would I be lettin' you out if I weren't? I'm doin' it mainly for the love I have for Gloria, I tell you. She doesn't know it quite yet, mind your smarts. But me heart's been hers ever since I first laid me eye upon the glorious vision of her clobberin' a cow with that club of hers. Ah, what a woman."

He touched a hand to his heart. "We figured it best to hide our little cahoots, wantin' to be safe and all. But I been working with her some months now. And so here I am, at your service. One eye or none, I'm the best you got."

Sera found herself trusting the man. Why *would* he let them go now if he wasn't on their side? Dak and Riq seemed to agree with her by the looks on their faces.

"So, what're we going to do?" Dak asked. "Should we just smash into the Amancios' room? Throw them overboard? Stop this thing before it even gets started?"

"Don't be as stupid as you look," Eyeball spat. "Do that and *we'll* be the ones accused of a mutiny. No, sir—we need to lie low until those turncoat brothers make their move against the captain. Then we come in and save the day. Every slimy-haired runt on this ship will know we're the heroes then."

Sera couldn't hide her worry. "That's the plan? What if the guards come down and see that we're gone? What if the Amancios do something bad to Columbus before we can save him? Slit his throat or poison him?"

"What if the moon cracks open and drops lamb chops on us?" Eyeball growled. "What if me legs fall off and start dancin'? We'll do our best, lad. Or should I say *lassie*?"

Sera's face colored. "Brute force just doesn't seem like the most thought-out plan is all."

Riq shrugged. "Sometimes you just need to go for it."

Eyeball huffed. "Are we really going to stand here like brain-dead flamingos and talk it over?"

"Like I said," Dak interjected. "Let's *do* this thing. I can barely stand it. If we're not going to do what the Hystorians sent us back to do, what's the point of being here? It's time to act, Sera."

She looked at him for a moment, then finally nodded.

"Right," Eyeball grunted. "Up we go."

They headed for the ladder.

They slipped past the guards at the top easily because they were snoring up a storm, practically lying on top of each other. Eyeball mentioned as they passed that he had helped them with their insomnia by pouring some powder into their drinks — a concoction he'd gotten from a mean old hag he'd met in the slums.

Valerian, probably, thought Sera, though her knowledge of medicinal herbs of the era was limited.

As they slunk their way through the narrow, cramped halls and corners of the ship's belly, she felt claustrophobic and nauseated and tired of the smells of body odor and foul breath. Soon enough, she told herself. Soon enough they'd be fighting for their lives in the wide open, nothing around them but air and sea.

They finally reached the hatch in the floor that led down to their short-lived sleeping quarters of the previous night. But instead of going down, Eyeball moved past it and stopped at a seemingly random spot farther along. He shushed them, then started running his fingers along the wood of the wall. There was a low grating sound and a panel popped out into his hands — he gently placed it on the ground.

"Weapons," he whispered.

Sera moved forward to stand beside him as he reached into the cubbyhole and pulled out knives and swords. She held her arms out and he stacked the weapons there like firewood. When the pile got heavy, Riq helped as well. In the end, there was an odd assortment of at least a dozen blades.

"Okay," Eyeball said, winking his lone eye. "Let's hope to the sea gods your Riffraff can swing these blasted things without choppin' their own ears off."

Sera nodded, then looked at Dak. It lifted her heart to see that his face was full of excitement more than fear. Maybe they could pull this off after all. Eyeball went down the ladder into the sleeping quarters first, then Dak. Riq got on his knees to pass the weapons to them — she saw Eyeball's large hands reach up and grab them. She followed Riq's lead, glad to be relieved of the burden.

When she looked back up she noticed her reflection in a tiny metal mirror hanging on the wall. At the sight of her face, a sudden and piercing ache seized her heart and squeezed it. She scooted backward until she hit the wall of the narrow hallway. A deep, black sadness filled her — a feeling she recognized all too well.

She was having a Remnant.

32

Stairway to Battle

IT DIDN'T last long, ending almost as suddenly as it had started. But the vision that passed through her mind—more like the *absence* of a vision, as if she were supposed to be seeing something but it wasn't there—haunted her deeply in those few seconds. In her mind's eye, she saw her face as it had appeared in the small mirror. And every ounce of her expected a woman's hands to appear and caress her cheeks, a beautiful face to reach down and kiss her forehead. The fact that it didn't happen was so maddening she thought she'd scream, or lose her mind completely. But then it was gone, just like that.

A Remnant. She'd had another Remnant.

She looked at Riq, realizing that she must look crazy.

"You okay?" he asked. His face revealed nothing.

"Yeah," she answered. "Yeah. I'm fine. Just . . . got spooked there for a second."

Dak called out from below. "You guys coming down or what?"

"Be right there," she whispered.

"Never mind," Dak returned. "We're coming up."

Sera glanced at Riq again, and he was giving her a knowing look.

"A Remnant?" he asked.

Sera tried to hide her surprise. Then she nodded.

"If we fix the Breaks, you won't have to deal with that anymore. Saving the world sounds great, but it's not a bad deal that we get to save ourselves in the bargain."

It was the nicest thing she'd heard him say. Not so much the words as the *way* he'd said it. Genuinely.

"Thanks," she whispered. A small echo of the pain she'd felt in that short burst of a few moments still lingered in her heart. But there wasn't any more time to dwell on it. Eyeball's head popped through the opening in the floor.

"Time for battle," he said.

Sera got the last pick of the lot from the weapons stash—but it wasn't too bad. A thin dagger about the length of her forearm. It ended in a vicious point and the blade along the side seemed freshly sharpened, the shiny silver surface almost glistening. It felt completely awkward in her hands. She took a few practice jabs and almost stabbed the only eye their new leader had left.

"Watch it, girl!" he barked. "Oops, now I guess they all know."

Most of the Riffraff army had climbed out of the

sleeping quarters, crowding the small hallway. Ricardo was nearby.

"You're a girl?" he asked. "For real?"

"For real," Sera said with a shrug of her shoulders. "But I can fight just like the rest of you."

"Never said you couldn't," he responded with a smile.

Sera felt the briefest disappointment that she'd probably never see the older boy again. She might have ended up liking him a lot—if only he weren't stinky and could travel through time.

"All right, this is how it's gonna happen," Eyeball said to the group. "We'll go wait right below the decks. The little pipsqueak Dak and I will climb up and watch for a signal that the Amancio brothers' plan is in motion. Then we'll all move in and rescue Captain Columbus. Easy as throwin' dice."

Sera felt like she had to question things one last time. "That's really it? Our only plan is to fight our way through a bunch of grown men—brandishing weapons we can hardly hold, much less use?"

"Yep," Eyeball responded with a grunt.

"Okay. Sounds good to me." She gave him a smile—a sudden confidence had filled her, though she had no idea where it came from. From the Remnant? A feeling that someone loved her and believed in her—even if it was someone she'd never met? Maybe. Either way, she'd take it.

"Then follow me," Eyeball said. He set off down the cramped hallway, and the Riffraff army went with him.

∞

Sera could smell the salty air as they got closer, could feel the coolness of it. She didn't care anymore if they had to fight with men twice her size—at least she'd be able to pull clean, crisp air into her lungs.

Eyeball stopped them at the foot of a steep, almost vertical wooden staircase that led up to the decks, then lined them up against the wall. Sera could see the stars through the hole at the top and she felt a rush of excitement. Dak was beside her, holding a curved sword that looked like it could chop heads off with ease.

"It's called a scimitar," he said. "Or it will be eventually, but they haven't actually coined the term yet. It originated in the Middle East, where—"

"Not now," Sera said. "Not now."

"Okay."

But his gaze didn't drop from her eyes, and a lot was said between them in the next couple of seconds without a word being spoken. That they were best friends; that they'd been through a lot and were about to go through their worst. But they were together and that made everything all right. They could do this.

Eyeball had climbed up the stairs until his head disappeared past the threshold. After looking in all directions, he crouched back down and called for Dak to come with him.

"Good luck," Sera said.

"Same to you. Remember, as soon as we know Columbus is safe, we need to get out of here. You be ready with that Ring."

"I will. It'll all be over soon."

Dak grinned. "Until we move on to the second Break and have to start all over."

"Right."

"Boy!" Eyeball roared—as much as he could while whispering. Somehow he managed it. "Get up here!"

Dak gave one last nod to Sera then scrambled up the stairs, almost face-planting into Eyeball's rear end before he realized how fast he was going. The two of them slipped into the night air and out of sight. A hush fell over everything.

Sera closed her eyes and enjoyed the clean feel of breathing the ocean air. She'd often heard people talk about the calm before the storm, and she finally knew what they'd meant. At any second, their world was going to explode into action.

Things began to happen.

There was a distant shout, the words impossible to make out. Then another. And another. A scuffling sound, then a bunch of voices at once, arguing. The ring of metal against metal. The quick *bang* of an explosion— someone had fired a musket. Sera had to restrain herself from sprinting up the stairs before their signal.

Suddenly the booming voice of Eyeball filled the air, turning her heart into a rattling alarm clock in her chest.

"Mutiny! Mutiny! Mutiny! Salvador and Raul are traitors! Rise up and fight!"

Dak's head popped through the opening at the top of the staircase.

"Riffraffs! It's time to fight!"

Mutiny on the *Santa María*

Dak scooted away from the opening as his small army started charging up the stairs and onto the deck. He got to his feet and turned to stand beside Eyeball again. The decks of the ship had been stone silent with no movement only a minute earlier. Now it was utter chaos, people running all over, fighting with swords and shooting muskets — though only a couple of people had those and it took forever to reload them after one shot. This battle would be won or lost by steel.

The problem was that the Amancio-led guards outnumbered the sailors who'd been brave enough to accept Eyeball's challenge to fight back. Hopefully the Riffraffs would turn that tide as they ran screaming in all directions, ready to distract those loyal to the Amancios while Eyeball took the fight to the brothers themselves. It was easy to see who was on whose side — the mutineers were big and strong with shiny weapons, while Dak's side looked pathetic and unorganized, with mismatched weapons and tattered clothing.

But he remembered the lesson of the American Revolution. In battle against an organized enemy, chaos could be effective. And the mutineers definitely hadn't been expecting this.

"Come with me," Eyeball said to Dak. "You and I are going for the big man himself. Columbus needs our help."

Sera stepped up beside them. "I'm coming, too."

Then Riq. "Don't forget me."

"All right. Just don't chicken out when the heads start flyin'," Eyeball said through a rumbling chuckle. "Come!"

Dak and the others followed as Eyeball ran forward, his stocky legs pumping as he jumped over ropes and buckets to charge toward the upper deck where the Amancio brothers were trying to break into the captain's quarters. Salvador wielded an axe, and one-third of the door was already shredded into splinters. A light rain had begun to fall from the dark sky, causing the lanterns that hung from masts and rafters to sputter and hiss. Dak could tell that the ship was bouncing more, too, and that the moon and stars had completely disappeared above them. The ship was heading straight into a storm.

The captain's cabin was on a raised deck that had a short flight of stairs on each side. At the bottom of each of them stood guards loyal to the Amancios, fighting off anyone and everyone who tried to gain access to the platform. Raul had just fired his musket at someone and was busily reloading, shoving a long metal rod down the barrel.

"No matter what happens," Eyeball said as they approached, "at least the world will know that those turncoat Amancios did in fact mutiny. Even if they win over this blasted ship, they've lost in the long run. Their heads'll be on pikes if they ever dare go back to Spain."

It hit Dak that they'd already made a difference by being there. They'd revealed the plot, and that alone could change how history evolved in the coming decades. But they couldn't leave anything to chance—they had to make sure the SQ didn't reach the New World. They had to.

The four of them rounded a large mast, and the platform of the captain's quarters loomed above them. Dak looked up to see that Raul had finished his preparation of the musket and was now aiming it directly at Eyeball.

"Watch out!" Dak shouted as he leapt to his left and knocked the man onto the deck, just as the short jolt of the gun's explosion ripped through the air. Dak heard the iron ball smash into the wood of the mast behind them.

"You'll all die for this!" Raul yelled. "All of you!"

Dak checked that Sera and Riq had found cover. He scampered to his feet and helped Eyeball get up as well.

"Thanks, lad," the man said. His lone eye gleamed with rage. "I'll fight to the death for you. Let's get those no-good brothers."

Dak nodded, a fire burning inside him—a courage he'd never felt before in his life. "One each, right?"

"Aye. One each. You go left, I'll go right."

Dak wasted no more time talking about it. He turned

and ran for the steps on the left side. A couple of Riffraff had ganged up on the guards at the bottom, swords ringing as they struck one another, the sailors slowly losing their ground. Sera and Riq joined Dak, and they slipped past the fight and bounded up the stairs.

Salvador was just pulling his axe back for another blow on the door when it suddenly burst open, shreds of wood flying everywhere, and Christopher Columbus came charging out with a sword. Eyeball was on the far side, by the other steps, trying to fight his way through a pair of guards. Raul had been preparing his musket for firing again but gave up, tossing it over the railing and pulling a knife from his belt. Dak went for him, screaming as he charged, raising his scimitar even though he had no real idea how to use the thing.

Raul stabbed at him when he approached but Dak swung his weapon downward, smacking the blade. It flew out of the man's grip and clanged against the hard wood of the deck. Dak felt a rush of pride, but Raul immediately came in with his other hand, squeezed into a fist, and punched Dak in the cheek. Pain exploded through his head, completely stunning him. Lights flashed before his eyes. He dropped his weapon and started falling, but someone caught him, pulled him back onto his feet.

It was Sera. He knew it even though he couldn't see her. Her arms were hooked under his, supporting him until he got his wits back. Riq had tackled Raul in the meantime, but the man pushed him off as Dak looked on. Riq smacked against the railing and let out a small cry. Dak put his weight back on his feet and Sera let go, stepping forward to stand beside him. Together they took in what was going on all around them.

To their left, Christopher Columbus was battling with Salvador, the steel of his blade clanging against the man's axe. Ahead of them, Eyeball had just clobbered a guard and was now charging forward to help the captain. To the right, below the deck on which they stood, Ricardo and his two friends were fighting a couple of guards, and they even seemed to be winning. Battles raged everywhere, and the Riffraff army was helping the sailors turn the tide against those loyal to the Amancios.

We just might win, Dak thought.

Lightning suddenly lit up the sky, its thunder booming almost immediately. The clouds opened up and rain fell in torrents. The ship rocked as if a big wave had just crashed into its side. Dak bumped into Sera and they both stumbled across the deck until they slammed into the wall of the cabin. Dak was able to right himself but Sera fell to the floor, right at the feet of Columbus, who appeared to be gaining the upper hand against Salvador — thanks to Eyeball, who'd attacked from the other side.

Dak was just about to reach down and help Sera when he heard a man shouting at the top of his lungs — the scream of a madman. Dak looked up to see Raul charging at him, his eyes filled with insane rage. Before he could react, the man tackled him, wrapping his arms around Dak's torso and throwing him to the ground. They hit the stairs and tumbled down, rolling over each other until they hit the bottom. Dak felt like every inch of his body had just been punched at once and his head spun with dizziness.

Raul's screams didn't stop. He gripped Dak even tighter and lifted him up, struggling to his feet as he held the boy in his arms. Dak squirmed and kicked—tried to free himself—but the man was too strong.

"I don't care what else happens," the Amancio brother shouted over the rain and thunder and sounds of battle. "But *you* will die! Tonight!"

Then, with another shriek of lunacy, the man ran forward to the railing of the ship and threw Dak over the side. Screams now erupting from his own throat, Dak plummeted into the dark depths of the stormy sea.

34

Breathless

THE OCEAN swallowed him.

It was cold—like a living creature of ice that bit every part of his body at once. He was dizzy and hurt and disoriented. Everything was dark and freezing and he couldn't tell what was up or down. His lungs screamed at him to breathe, to take in air—now, now, now! But he overpowered the urge, knew that he if he did so he'd only pull in water and drown. So he struggled, kicked, and flailed, tried to push himself to the surface, hoping that he'd naturally go in the right direction.

A pain throbbed in his skull. His insides felt as if they might explode. He scissored his legs in the thick water, pulled at it with his arms. The need for air became all powerful, an inferno that roared in his heart and through his veins, squeezing his lungs as if someone had wrapped ropes around them and were cinching them tighter and tighter. He wanted to scream, but knew that would be the end, too.

He broke through the water's rough surface.

After sucking in a huge gulp of air, he sputtered and spit out the seawater that came in with it. Pumping his arms and legs to tread in the choppy ocean, he stuck his mouth as high as he could to breathe. Lightning still ripped white, jagged streaks in the sky above, and the rain lashed at his face. His body felt like it was stuck on a slow-motion trampoline that just wouldn't stop, the sea moving him up and then down again, up and then down again. And the cold. He was already losing feeling in his hands and feet.

He twisted around to see that the ship was about a hundred feet away, its lanterns' glow eerie in the midst of the storm. With the rain and the bobbing of the waves and the lightning flashes making the darkness more stark when they vanished, it was hard to tell how the battle was going. But he caught the silhouette of a man standing straight and tall at the railing, looking right at him. And he knew who it was.

Christopher Columbus.

They'd done it. They'd really done it. Too bad Dak was going to celebrate by getting eaten by sharks. Or drowning. He couldn't decide which was worse.

"Dak!"

Impossibly, he heard a voice coming from somewhere nearby. Still treading with all of his strength, he looked around, straining to see through the darkness and pounding rain. There was another flash of lightning and he saw a small boat just a dozen feet away, its occupants rowing mightily. Sera. Riq. Eyeball, his namesake body part seeming to glow as it stared him down.

Pure elation filled Dak from top to bottom. He waved a hand into the wet air. "I'm here! Right here!"

"We know, you idiot!" Eyeball roared with a laugh.

Sera leaned forward to be heard over the storm. "We did it! Salvador is dead and his brother was thrown overboard right after you! Columbus is in charge and the battle's over!"

Dak's heart leapt at the news. And it had never felt so good to see his—

Someone grabbed him from behind, gripping an arm around his neck like a vice. Dak gasped, beat at the thick muscles of the forearm that had begun squeezing the life out of him.

"Dak!" Sera yelled. "Dak!" She was helpless on the boat, could do nothing but shout his name.

"I told you," a man whispered into his ear. "I said you'd die, and now you will. You and me both."

Raul.

Dak could barely breathe. He kicked his legs below him, trying to hit the man in the knee. He pulled and swatted at his arm, but nothing worked. He was choking, and once again his lungs begged for air.

"Down we go," Raul said.

Then he pulled Dak under the water, just as Sera yelled his name again.

Cold water. Blackness. Pain in his neck, his head. Pain all over. No air, his chest screaming for it. The sheer desperation of it all shot a burst of adrenaline surging through his body and he went ballistic, punching and squirming like a rabid animal until he somehow got free. His head broke the surface again and he sucked in a breath, but he knew the madman would be on him again in seconds.

"Sera!" he yelled hoarsely. "Use the Infinity Ring! Take us out of here! Now!"

They were close, but not close enough to help. Sera's face was a mask of fear as she leaned over the edge of the boat, reaching helplessly for him.

Dak felt movement behind him, a hand sliding up his back, reaching for his neck.

"Sera!" Dak shouted.

Raul pulled him back below the water. Dak barely got in another breath before it happened. An arm slipped around his neck again, squeezing even tighter than before. Dak's eyes bulged open, but he saw nothing. Only black water. His mouth opened up and the cold liquid rushed in; he spit it out. He gripped the man's arm with both hands but knew it was pointless now. He kicked out with his legs because he had nothing else.

Lights began to dance before his eyes. Numbness filled his chest, replacing the pain. His throat was doing funny things as he fought the urge to suck in a breath of pure salt water, which would fill his lungs and kill him.

In that moment, death waiting to take hold, he thought of his parents. He closed his eyes, and in his mind he saw that goofy look on his dad's face when he'd unveiled a new invention. He saw the sweetness in his mom's eyes after she'd kissed him on the fore-head before saying good night. He saw that last glimpse of them he'd had before they'd been sucked into the wormhole, vanishing into time itself.

He saw them, and almost felt their presence. He decided it was time to quit fighting. He was floating now. He sensed people grabbing at his shirt, pulling on it. But it was too late. Death began to drag him down.

The last thing he saw was a whirlpool of lights.

35

Changes

BRINT SAT brooding in the tiny office of the Hystorians' fallback shelter, staring at an old class photo hanging on the wall. He was still depressed, but he felt he had good reason to be.

They'd lost their headquarters. There was no salvaging it once the SQ had descended upon them. They'd barely survived the attack, and not without some heavy losses. The men and women that had gotten away were now regrouping here, at their hideaway across town. Thank goodness they always planned for the worst.

At least Dak, Sera, and Riq had gotten away safely, and with the Infinity Ring. Not only did it mean they had hope of Aristotle's grand plan finding success, but the time-travel device itself was far away from the reaches of their enemy. At least in the present day.

Mari came in, a raised bruise forming on her cheek. "You okay?" she asked.

"Well enough." Brint looked back at the photo, not sure why it had him so mesmerized—he'd glanced at that thing a million times before. "How about you?"

"I'm fine. Why are you staring at the wall like that?"

"Huh?" His gaze moved to her. "Oh. Sorry. Just . . ."

An odd feeling came over him—pleasant but unexpected. Indescribable. He stood up and walked over to where the photo hung and took it off the nail, held it up to inspect it. Columbus High School, top of his class. It had been twenty-five years. Hard to believe.

"Did you know my school was named after Christopher Columbus?" he asked Mari.

"Of course. Who else would it be named after?"

Brint shrugged. "I don't know. I guess I'm just having good memories of my time there. Forget it." He put the photo back in its place, straightened it. Then he turned to face his longtime partner. "What do you think? About today?"

"I think we had some lucky breaks. And we survived to fight another day."

"Always finding the positive, aren't you?" Brint asked.

"Well, who knows. Maybe for once time's on our side."

Time Out

SERA HAD saved her best friend from drowning. He *so* owed her.

She sat on the edge of an old wooden pallet, in the middle of a dark and dusty place that looked like a warehouse of some sort. It's where she'd appeared after pulling Dak out of the ocean and warping herself, Dak, and Riq away from the storm. They lay next to her, all three of them sopping wet.

She shivered from the cold and looked around. Streams of light broke through slats and holes in the ceiling, the glowing beams full of dancing motes. The place was dank and smelled of old wine. Barrels and caskets and boxes littered countless rickety shelves.

"Where are—" Dak began to whisper, but then he cut off and scrambled to his feet. He sprinted across the dirty floor of the warehouse before Sera could ask him what he was doing. She grabbed Riq's hand and pulled him up, then they both ran after Dak.

He'd come to a stop at the door to the place. A poster

had been nailed to its surface, with an artist's pencil drawing of a man and a woman standing side by side, staring glumly at whomever might look back. Below their picture, a phrase was scrawled in big black letters, but in another language—Sera knew it must be French.

Dak was frozen. Sera couldn't breathe. Riq glanced back and forth between them, confused.

"Those are Dak's parents," Sera whispered.

"What does it . . ." Dak began to ask.

Riq's face had gone pale. He cleared his throat. Then he translated.

"Wanted. For crimes against the Revolution."